SILVER SERIES

SUPERB WRITING
TO FIRE THE IMAGINATION

Tanith Lee writes, 'Old legends have it that, before men became kings, women ruled large areas of the world. They were as powerful and as ruthless as any of the man-ruled states which came after. Indeed, the harshness of men towards women in many early societies was, they said, due to the cruelty the female societies – matriarchies – had already displayed towards men.

And so what happens if a young man from a male-dominant world gets thrown into a world of matriarchy? Fascinated by that thought, I set out to explore the whole thing in this novel.'

Tanith began writing when she was nine and has not stopped since. With 17 children's books, 43 adult novels, 8 short story collections, four radio plays and two episodes of the cult television series *Blake's Seven* to her name, she has won the World Fantasy Award twice and the August Derleth Award. The first story in the *Wolf Tower* sequence – *Law of the Wolf Tower* – was shortlisted for the Guardian Children's Fiction Award.

EAST OF MIDNIGHT

Tanith Lee

Hodder
Children's
Books

A division of Hodder Headline Limited

Contents

To Marni

Part One

Part One

ONE

The Slave

Dekteon opened his eyes. He saw upward, through his own red hair, a red-burning autumn wood, and beyond that a cold red sunrise. He was lying on his side. He had slept in this position, and now he ached with stiffness. His immediate thought was for the dogs. He listened, heard nothing. It was disturbing. The last thing he remembered was being under the stone slab, in the rank darkness, the dogs belling overhead . . . and yet, he was above ground now, in this wood, which he did not recall entering, and the sun was rising.

Dekteon slowly stood up, rubbing life back into limbs and body. The day was frosty, very still. No birds sang.

The noise, when it came, was sharp and unnerving through the trees. A cart appeared suddenly, drawn by a roan horse. There was something odd about the cart – its shape, something. Dekteon could not be sure. A hooded man drove the cart, hunched over the reins. Dekteon thought the man had not seen him, but the cart drew to a halt. There was something about the horse, too. It was stocky, broader in the chest and heavier in the head than any horse Dekteon had seen before. Its legs—

'Come,' the man in the hood called abruptly. He could only be speaking to Dekteon. A white glimpse of face showed in the hood, turned towards him. 'Come, hurry and get in.'

Dekteon was afraid. Could his master have sent this man to find him? No. If the dogs had not caught him on the hills, this one man would be no good at it, even with his peculiar cart and the peculiar horse. He looked like a foreigner, and he spoke in a stilted over-precise way. And yet, most curiously, there was something familiar about him.

'Come,' the foreign man called again. 'Hurry.'

Dekteon assumed a boldness he did not feel.

'I don't know you. What do you want with me?'

'You are stayed for. My master wishes you to hurry.'

'Who is your master?' Dekteon demanded. His throat was dry. 'Is it Lord Fren of By-the-Lake?'

'No. Hurry. You are stayed for.'

The horse shook its head. Beads flashed on the bridle. Its feet were unshod, not horse's feet at all, but more like the pads of a bear.

A shiver rattled up Dekteon's spine. Definitely not one of the horses of Lord Fren.

'You have no other place to go to,' the pale man said.

That was true enough.

Dekteon swallowed. His back gnawed in the cold from Lord Fren's final beating, and when he moved the raw scars tore like cloth. Out here, with no food or shelter, he would not last long.

'All right, I'll come with you. But if you mean me any harm I'll kill you. I'm an escaped slave – you know as much, don't you? So I've nothing to lose.'

The words seemed ominous to Dekteon, even as he hauled himself up into the cart behind the hooded man.

There was a thick pelt on the floor of the cart, and a packet of cold meat and a stoppered jar of drink, as if waiting for him. Dekteon looked at these things suspiciously, but he was starved, had been two days with emptiness in his belly. Soon he ate the meat, and drank from the jar. There appeared nothing unusual about the jar, or the vinegary flat ale it contained.

Dekteon lay back on the pelt, his hand on the bit of filed metal in his belt that served as a knife. He determined not to sleep. He wondered muzzily where the hooded man was taking him.

Dekteon would end badly, he had always known it. The old slave in the Shore House at By-the-Lake had warned him often and often. But Dekteon was young and strong, and he had red hair, a red dark as baked terracotta clay. Hard, maybe, to be a slave with such hair, even when you were born to slavery.

Still, the hair had made a handy tag for his masters to remember him by, more convenient than his given name. He had been in three households, and named 'Red' in each. 'Red! Fetch the logs, and move more swiftly, you lazy devil.' 'Red, you have not oiled this strap sufficiently.' 'Get me that red dog. He's due a whipping.'

Dekteon had been a slave-woman's child; slaves were

not permitted any form of marriage, and he had never known his father. He had dwelt ten years in a prosperous southern household, a mansion. The Hall had been very large, with a great central chimney. Silk gleamed on the walls. He had glimpsed this from the doorway but never entered. The slaves' quarters were mean, and their possessions few. The lord had a garden with black-green trees cut into grotesque shapes, and a round pool with golden fish in it. When he was eight, Dekteon had caught one of these fish. That had been the occasion of his first whipping. He had been made dog boy, looking after the lord's hounds, but when he was ten, this lord had begun feuding with another. Presently the mansion was sacked and the slaves randomly carried off. His mother had been taken in another direction. He never saw her again.

He served his new master till he was seventeen. At thirteen, he had been branded. They thrust a piece of rag between your teeth to stop you biting your tongue when the iron touched you, also to muffle the cries. Dekteon had stood in a line of boys at the smithy forge. Each had their mouths stuffed with rag. The white-hot iron sizzled. Each screamed, and the rag fell out. Dekteon had willed himself not to scream, but he had. It was like another person shouting out, using his voice. The brand was in the shape of two small wings with a bar across them, a typical Lakeland slave-brand, meaning *This bird cannot fly*. When he was seventeen, his master had lost him in a wager on a chariot race. He went to Lord Fren, at the Shore House in By-the-Lake.

Dekteon was born and bred a slave; he knew what

was expected of him and what was not, but somehow he had never quite learned, as a slave should. He had tended horses and dogs, felled wood, gone wolf-hunting, run long distances. He was strong and became stronger, being much in the open air. The other slaves grumbled among themselves, slunk about and squabbled in dark corners, trembled or fawned when the masters came near. Dekteon would let the master call two or three times before he ran to him. When he respectfully bowed, he made much of it, almost a pantomime. Inside himself, unvoiced and virtually unrecognised, an anger was building. And this anger showed itself in idiot bravado. He stole from the lord's kitchen, and his orchard; poached his woods, tickled fish from his streams. He would ride Lord Fren's black stallion in the stable-yard, and one day Lord Fren caught him at it. Dekteon was beaten. A slave got used to beatings, though this was one of the worst. Next morning, Fren, coming in an ill mood from a quarrel with his First Wife, stuck one too many spurs in the stallion and it threw him in the mud. Dekteon was blamed. He had harmed the horse, bewitched it. The old slave, apparently careless of his own safety, came to warn Dekteon that another beating was in store. Dekteon realised that another beating would be too much. Even his resilient body had taken enough of the rod for the time being. He panicked. He hid in the hay barn, a stupid, unimaginative thing to do. Soon Fren's pompous steward found him. Then Dekteon did the ultimate stupid thing: he fought the steward's men, knocked out the steward's teeth; somehow a lamp overturned and the barn was set ablaze. At length,

Dekteon was felled from behind. A little later, he got the second beating.

Afterwards, when he was lying feverish and sick from it in the out-house where kindling was stored, the old slave had crept in to him again. Dekteon had never learned the old man's name, nor his duties. He did not even eat with the other slaves, nor share their haphazard pursuits. Sometimes Dekteon would not see him for days, yet he always seemed to want to help if there was trouble. Or, at least, offer his rather irritating advice. Now, however, he was truly practical. He had brought water in a cup, but Fren's bully, guarding the door, had jostled him so most of the water was spilled. As Dekteon gulped what was left, the old slave told him Fren's plan. The disobedient red dog was to be sold to the copper mines.

It was a death sentence, but one which would bring his master cash. For a strong slave was worth a lot to the mines. He might last all of two years there, before the unspeakable conditions killed him.

Dekteon lay in the filthy straw, his eyes wide and unseeing. He no longer felt his pain or illness, only absolute despair, which was worse than either.

The old slave leaned over him, and put a chunk of bread into his jacket, and sliced through his rope bindings with a spike of sharp filed iron. Dekteon was amazed. It revived him. He stared at the old man who said quietly, 'They think you're too weak to get away now, and you are, but you must try. Only one man at the door, and dark soon, and dinner. Make for the Round Hill, and over.'

'But—' Dekteon said. 'Where can I go?'

The old slave looked strange, almost clever. His eyes glimmered.

'Follow the uplands. Three, four hills, a night's journey. There is a ring of stones, sunken, an old place. Nearby a river. Cross. Other side is wild land, many outlaws – safe. When I was young,' the old slave chanted, 'two or three ran from this house and went that way, and Fren's father never caught them.'

In his fever, Dekteon was stimulated by the wild notion of escape. Presently, the old man put the iron in Dekteon's belt and went away.

Even here, Dekteon could smell the roast meat from the Hall, and the smoke of new-lit lamps. Someone brought food for Dekteon's guard. As he was eating it, Dekteon slunk out of the door behind him, a log from the wood-store in his hand. He smashed the log on the guard's head, then propped him against the door of the out-house, as if he were asleep. Dekteon had been afraid to use the improvised iron knife. He had never killed a man. No one was about in the yard, and there was a place in the wall he knew of, where he could get through. He had perhaps an hour, two if he were lucky, before the guard roused or was discovered.

The fever made Dekteon buoyant at first.

He ran, under the star-freckled sky, tasting hope.

All night he ran, or stumbled, over hills, along overgrown tracks. But somehow he had lost the meal of bread, and when the sun rose, he knew himself sick and shattered, as if the light revealed it to him.

Everything became a blur of hurt and chill heat, through which he shambled doggedly onward. He did not see the ring of stones till noon, and by then he had distinguished hounds giving tongue behind him. He was to be hunted down, and maybe torn in pieces.

Then he reached the stones. They were lopsided, ugly. They had a make-shift look, leaning there against the grim blowing sky of autumn, yet probably they had been there centuries or more. From the slope, crazy with fear, Dekteon had looked back and seen twenty dogs racing small as ants up the landscape towards him, men on horses riding after. He heard the shouts and baying clear as fate in the air.

He ran among the stones. He could not make out a river anywhere, near or far. Something tripped him and he crashed down. It was a great granite slab, shaggy with moss, half pushed up from the earth at the centre of the stone ring.

A foolish thought came to Dekteon. If he lifted the slab aside, there would be an area beneath which would conceal him. Ludicrous. How could he know such a thing? Besides, how could he summon the strength to move the stone?

The noise of the dogs got louder. Dekteon set his hands on the granite slab and began frantically – insanely – trying to shift it. And somehow, insanely, he found the strength, and the stone began to alter its position.

Now he could see into a narrow black hole beneath, just wide enough to contain a man. Shuddering with fatigue and terror, Dekteon jumped down into this blackness – which might have been the entry to some bottomless abyss, but luckily was not. His feet hit a floor instantly. The hole was about six feet deep. He reached and wrestled with the slab above. And the slab seemed to return easily, obligingly, into its former site, covering him.

Within the black was profound silence. The belling of the dogs came faintly, as if from a vast distance.

Dekteon felt dizzy. He slumped against the side of the blackness and shut his eyes.

He woke in a red wood at sunrise, to a cart, and a horse with the feet of a bear.

Dekteon started up in the cart. Had he fallen asleep? Fool, he must not; yet he had. The wood had thinned. The sun was older, already past the noon zenith, an opaque yellow. It was growing misty.

The hooded man was still driving, still hunched forward. The bizarre horse padded softly on. Dekteon's sore back burned. He winced, and leaned forward to the driver.

'You never said where we were going.'

'To my master,' the man said at once.

'Who is that?'

'My master's name is Zaister.'

Dekteon tried to order his wits.

'Why does he want me? How did you know where to find me?'

'You were expected.'

Could it be, Dekteon wondered, that he had somehow discovered and crossed the river after all, while he was delirious, and now he was in outlaw country, being taken to some petty chieftain? Best to keep quiet for the moment, if so. Certainly, the hooded man did not seem familiar any more. Dekteon had better see how the land lay before he asked anything else. And he would not sleep again.

The mist was getting thicker. The russet horse faded into it; the stands of trees vanished.

The wheels of the cart made a dull grinding, the beaded bridle chinked; there was no other sound.

They went on like this, in the mist, with no word spoken and no landmark, presumably for a couple of hours. For some reason he could not fathom, the mist alarmed Dekteon. Perhaps because it seemed a natural symbol of his own confusion. But then, as suddenly as it had seemed to accumulate, the mist began to disperse, unwinding in long scarves from about the cart.

They bounced over a slope, and down the other side. They were on a paved track. How had the hooded man identified the track, let alone kept to it in the mist?

A valley opened ahead and to both sides, clear to its edges and rimmed with a soft blaze of trees. There was a town in the valley, but as they went further, Dekteon saw it was deserted and in ruins. The roofs had fallen, though the stone walls yet stood. Between the houses, wild sheep were grazing on the brown grass. They had matted curling black fleece and wide eyes. They glared at the cart as it went by, without running away. At the north-western end of the valley was a bluish hill capped by earthworks. Not much remained of the lord's stronghold that had stood there: four look-out towers, a wall, the dilapidated mansion itself. The cart followed the track straight through the valley, up the hill and the earthworks, and in at the gate-less gateway. An avenue of weather-pocked statuary led to the mansion door, lions without heads and winged dogs with lichen growing from their jaws.

The cart stopped by the doorway. A slender tree was growing from an ancient well in the yard.

The hooded man got down from the box.

'Come,' he said to Dekteon, just as he had before. 'Hurry.'

In about two hours, from the look of it, the sun would set again. Westering, it struck inside that hood. The man's face was really extraordinarily white. Not unhealthy, simply colourless. The eyes, too, were curiously bright, almost phosphorescent in the hood's shadow.

Dekteon left the cart, reluctantly. He was unsure what would happen next. 'Come,' White-Face repeated. 'Follow me. You are stayed for.'

He went in at the doorway where once there had been a door, now gone. Dekteon glanced around. Now might be the last chance to make a break. No other outlaws were about, no other strangers with luminous eyes.

Something made him look up.

A bird hung in the sky above him, black on broad wings, motionless. It seemed to be watching him. A ridiculous fancy, yet one he could not dismiss. Dekteon shrugged, a fatalistic gesture that did not hearten him. He followed White-Face in at the Hall door.

If it was an outlaw hold, it was a weird one. With no outlaws. With nobody. Except, of course, for White-Face, and the invisible master, Zaister.

Dekteon had caught himself considering if it would

13

be more enjoyable being the slave of Zaister than the slave of Fren. But then, Zaister had not bought him, did not even claim him. In fact, in the oddest way, Dekteon was being treated as a guest.

The Great Hall of the ancient house was a wreck. At the northern end the rounded flank of another tower swelled into the mansion. The wooden door to the tower was present, and shut, though it had no visible lock. Stairs led down into a shambles of kitchen. The spits, the ovens, everything was crumbling, and somehow unfinished-looking. The chimney above the central hearth must obviously be clotted with rubble, rubbish and soot, and no fire had been lit beneath. However, a bronze brazier stood nearby. Soon White-Face had ministered to it and coals glowed, giving off a luxurious pulsing heat. There was something peculiar about the brazier, too. What was it?

White-Face produced meat and a loaf from bins, and another ration of the sour ale, setting them on a table. Dekteon, unable to think of anything more sensible to do, began to eat.

'Blood on your clothes,' stated White-Face.

'I was beaten,' Dekteon mumbled, surprised it should be mentioned. Next second he was more surprised. His jacket and shirt had been ripped off his back. Startled, Dekteon leapt up. White-Face waved him down. He went to yet another bin and produced a crock of glaucous stuff. 'For healing,' he calmly said.

Dekteon sat uneasily and let White-Face smear the medicine on his weals. Awesomely, the pain vanished immediately.

14

'I thought,' Dekteon said, 'I was to hurry.'

'There is time now, before sunset. Plenty of time now.'

'What happens at sunset, then? Is that when I meet – your master?' Dekteon was glad that he had stopped himself saying '*our* master'.

White-Face did not answer. Instead he said, 'I will bring fresh clothing. You will put it on.'

'All right.'

White-Face went out again.

Dekteon, despite himself, revelled in the warmth, the food, the termination of his pain. He finished the meat and rubbed the grease up from the plate with the last of his bread. He up-ended the cup of ale into his mouth to get every drop. As a slave, you learned to be thorough. Even comfort you learned to take where you could.

Funny, that brazier. What *was* it? Like the cart, not quite right. And that horse – but perhaps the horse was only some domesticated beast exclusive to this particular area. A slave was as ignorant of geography and wildlife as he was of most things. Who was to say there were not herds of bear-footed horses in this district, and quite normal?

Dekteon's hair crawled nervously. He knew at once he was being watched. Cautious, he rose, moving as if to warm himself at the brazier. Spinning suddenly about, he saw no one. The doorway of the kitchen was empty, the stairway beyond, empty, too. Dekteon went back up the stairs a little way, and stared at the wooden door in the rounded wall of the tower. It was shut. Besides, he would have heard footsteps on the stairs. Dekteon recollected the bird hanging in the sky.

TWO

Full Moon

Dekteon went back into the kitchen and sat down. White-Face returned a minute later, as unostentatiously as he had gone.

White-Face had brought clothes, as he had said he would. Dekteon wondered if this were some joke. For one thing, the garments were very fine; for another, they were all red. Red shirt, red tunic, red breeches. Boots of red bull's hide and a belt of the same with burnished bronze studs. There was embroidery on the tunic done in gold thread, a bizarre design of discs and antlered beasts like stags. Of course, a mighty lord might dress his slaves richly, but this Zaister would not be a mighty lord, not living here in this ruin. And Dekteon was not Zaister's slave.

'Your master jests,' Dekteon said. He made no move to put on the clothes. White-Face's own were unexotic: grey homespun trousers, a hooded tunic.

'Hurry,' White-Face said. 'In half of one hour the sun will set.'

'It's no matter to me,' Dekteon said, though his flesh

crawled again. The sense of being spied-on had not lessened.

White-Face said, 'Your garments are dirty and ragged. These garments are warm and pleasant. You would like to wear them.'

'Would I? No, I don't think I would. I don't think I like anything about them, or you, or your lord's house.' Dekteon, losing his head, was growing heated. 'As for your master, he doesn't own me. I'm a runaway; no one owns me now. I'm – I'm *free* –' Dekteon faltered, stunned by this astounding truth.

But a voice said from the doorway, 'None of us is free.'

Dekteon jerked about, and what he saw shut his mouth.

'None of us,' the man said again. 'King, lord, master, servant. We are all slaves to something. I am Zaister. And you, my friend, have drunk more ale than you're used to.'

He was young this man, this Zaister, two or three years older than Dekteon, maybe. He was well-built, of Dekteon's height, and summer-tanned as Dekteon was. His face was handsome and had the look on it a man's face will get when he has been in pain a long while and knows the pain will only get worse. The effect of his face and his look was almost overpowering to Dekteon, the sense of colliding with another human life. But it was not only this. The man wore scarlet bordered with saffron. Across his shoulders was slung, almost negligently, a collar of red-gold. His hair was the same colour as the gold.

Dekteon had an impulse, one he had never had before, to accept Zaister as his lord. Dekteon's first master and his second had been much alike, with their stupid faces, balding pates, pudgy hands. Fren had had a pot-belly and a soft pink mouth. If Zaister had been his master, Dekteon would have served him. It was that simple and that unnerving. Dekteon resented what he felt.

'You see,' Zaister said, 'what I ask you to wear is no more lavish than my own gear.'

'What happens at sunset?' Dekteon asked. It was an effort.

Zaister's eyes fixed on Dekteon. Masters never saw slaves. Even when they personally beat you, somehow, they never saw. Zaister saw, right through into the mind beyond the gaze. He knows he can make me obey him, Dekteon thought, make me obey without threat or blow, because I want to.

'At sunset,' Zaister said, 'the night comes. You are to be my night-watchman. Until midnight is passed, at least.'

'If I refuse?' Dekteon said.

Zaister went on observing him intently. Quietly, Zaister said, 'Why should you? Here you'll receive food and shelter. No one seeks to return you to the house of your rightful owner. If you leave here, where would you go? Do you have a family or friends, an inheritance, land, some provision for your future? No. You have a hungry trek across hostile country. You have the certainty that few will dare aid you, that inevitably the slave-brand will be noticed, there on your left shoulder where I notice it now. And then it will be the mines for you, or more probably the end of a rope.'

Dekteon shifted warily, pointlessly, like an animal in a cage.

'If I'm your watchman, what do I look out for?'

'For danger. For enemies. What else?'

'Perhaps I'll go in the night, or fall asleep. Perhaps I won't be much use as a watchman.'

'It's hard to sleep here,' Zaister said. 'Tonight is full moon, a white night. I recommend the new clothes. Your shirt is in two pieces, the ends trailing on the floor. It's bitter outside.'

Zaister turned and went from the kitchen. His footsteps were almost silent. The door of the tower opened, almost silent, too, then closed.

Dekteon stripped, took up the red garments and put them on. His back felt as if it had never been scored. The clothes fitted as if made for him. White-Face stood impassively by, and his eyes glowed in the shadow of his hood.

Three watch-towers faced south-east; one loomed to the west. All were ruinous. The wall ran between them, here and there pierced by gateways empty of gates or by large holes. Anything could get in at any time, and probably did. On top of the wall was a parapet, and a broad walk-way. Every yard or so the wall was choked with fallen bricks or weeds, passable only by scrambling. In places the footing looked unsafe. There were also remnants of walls on the inside of the courtyard, and the remains of a granary, smithy, bakehouse, and similar buildings. South-west and north-west a wild walled garden erupted trees.

Certainly, it was like any lord's mansion, fallen into massive disrepair. And yet, like all the rest, there was something about the dismal decaying edifice that seemed improbable . . . more as if it had never been properly begun than that it was rotting away from neglect and age. And then, that avenue of statues – winged dogs and lions with snakes' tails – he had never seen such a thing before. The towers had curious roofs, sloping sharply up in a wedge shape, not like the towers of the Lakeland, or of any hold Dekteon had come across. Additional items bothered Dekteon, foolish items. The too-vibrant crimson of some trees, the searing yellow of others, more like a tapestry depicting autumn than the season itself.

The sky, cloudless and cold, had turned to a lavender dome, resting on the barricades of mist that were stealing in from the edges of the valley. The setting sun was enormously sinking behind the western tower. No birds flew or cried.

Down on the valley plain, half a mile away, the black sheep were still cropping the grass between the empty stone houses. Even the sheep were wrong. Black and curly, glaring and unafraid. Noiseless.

Dekteon pulled close the red woollen cloak White-Face had handed him. He knew his duties. Watch till moonset, moving when and where he thought best, but taking in walls, courtyard, the mansion itself. Only Zaister's tower did not require his vigilance.

'And if I see anything, what?' Dekteon had demanded of the pale servant.

The servant said nothing, which was unsatisfactory, but final. Dekteon gave up.

He cursed himself, and stamped his new boots against the chill. A bit of brick snapped off at the vibration and plummeted the sixty feet down from the wall. Dekteon scowled after it. He would probably be killed before long. The wall would collapse under him. He glanced at Zaister's tower. The unfamiliar wedge-shaped roof rose from the flat roof of the house. Dekteon expected a light to appear in the tower, now the sun was going, but no light came. No lights came anywhere. No stars, even, above.

Dekteon could smell the gathering mist, but no other smell; not even smoke, or grass. He began to patrol the queasy wall.

Two hours after sunset, the moon rose in the east.

A full moon, as Zaister had said, pure white, almost blinding. The valley had become a bowl of mist, which the moon changed to milk. The hill and its earthworks poked above the mist like an island from a sea.

Dekteon had been around the whole circumference of the wall, pausing to examine the watch-towers thoroughly. Everything was quiet. Nothing moved. No birds nested in the towers, no mice traced the dust of the old granary. A stagnant pool somewhere in the overgrown garden made a faint glutinous noise as a trickle of hidden fountain ran into it. Odd that a fountain should play when the wells were dry. No lamps were lit in the house, or Zaister's tower.

Despite himself, uncanny stories began to crowd in

21

on Dekteon, slave superstitions. The ruin was nothing if not eerie, and somehow the moon's rising, which might have been expected to dispel night-fears, accentuated them.

Dekteon leaned on a stout area of parapet, watching the moon come over the mist. Now he was remembering a fragment of song from his childhood. The men had sung it in the slaves' hall. It had been a feast day, and there had been a beer ration. Dekteon recalled the flash of firelight on iron mugs and big roaring mouths. A song about a quarrel between a man and a woman, but the moon was in it too . . .

The moon walks east of midnight,
The sun walks west of noon.
And though I love you, sweetheart,
I will not sing your tune.

Dekteon found himself whistling the song, but the whistle came too loud in the utter stillness all about.

He turned abruptly and went down the wall-stair towards the courtyard, meaning to get some ale to warm himself. There was no trace of danger in this uninhabited moon-bright night. Besides, he was not Zaister's slave, to stay at his post, hour on hour.

Near the foot of the stair, Dekteon hesitated. His heart gave a huge lunge, practically stifling him. Something was standing in the courtyard. A dark squat thing – facing him, for he caught the glint of its eyes.

It had four legs, it was an animal. A wolf? No, not a wolf.

Dekteon gave a snap of laughter.

22

He ran down the last stairs. It was one of the wild sheep, got in at the open gate. Dekteon waved his arms, running straight at the sheep. Which did not move.

Dekteon stopped again, for this was absurd. Sheep always ran away; they were cowardly, silly. Not this one, though. This one stood motionless, its eyes fixed on him, the moon striking down on it. The curled fleece looked like a thousand black and white crescents carved on its back.

Dekteon felt embarrassed. He had never been a shepherd, and did not know what to do with the sheep, which plainly was not intimidated.

'Come,' Dekteon said, trying to reason with it.

He went forward again. He would have to drive the sheep outside. It should not be here.

Behind the sheep, the avenue of statues burned in moonlight.

'Go on,' Dekteon suggested. He put out his hand to touch the sheep, and suddenly, ridiculously, knew he was afraid of it as it was not afraid of him.

Dekteon drew back his hand. The sheep's gelid eyes gleamed. It turned slowly, and went slowly back into the avenue, along it, and out of the empty gateway. Dekteon was trembling, too scared yet for shame.

He crossed the yard, went in at the house door, and through the shadowy hall. The moon did not strike so far. It was a relief to be out of the moonlight, as out of too strong sun.

The moon walks east of midnight, the sun walks west of noon. Nonsense words, that didn't mean anything.

Dekteon went down into the kitchen. No lamp there,

either, but the brazier of coals still burned, and by its faint illumination he found the jar of ale, and poured a measure and drank it, and then another and drank that, too. The ale steadied him. Idiot, to fear, of all things, a *sheep*.

There was a crash.

It sounded so loud, it might have been part of the house tumbling.

Dekteon had dropped the earthenware cup. Now he took a step and the pieces scrunched like bones under his feet.

The crash had come from the north-west side of the house, out of the wild garden. Probably it was nothing, a stone toppling. Whatever else, no one but he had roused.

Dekteon searched briefly in the kitchen for the spike of filed metal the old slave had provided him. Unable to locate it, or any other improvised weapon, he went reluctantly into the passage White-Face had shown him, which led directly to the garden. The passage ended in a small door, warped and difficult to shift. Masked from the kitchen by an angle of wall, the passage itself was pitch black, but the door gave suddenly and moonlight exploded through.

There was an ancient kitchen garden there, or had been, screened off from the formal garden by another area of wall. Dekteon climbed over the wall, which had mostly come down.

The garden was hushed, innocent. The lawns had grown as high as his knees. The trees were grey now, with thin black cypresses towering between them. Not seeing the steps in the undergrowth, Dekteon almost fell. At the bottom, water shone muddily. The fountain which he had heard earlier jetted from a stone mask on a pillar. The face of the mask was held in a ghastly, yawning pop-eyed rigour, as if it were about to vomit.

Nowhere could he see any evidence of the thing which had crashed.

Then the crash came again, so close to him he nearly sprang from his skin.

Shaken but determined, Dekteon forced his way through the grass and between the rogue roots of trees. He came into the open before a pavilion, the sort of little shrine many lords put up to a garden spirit. The roof of the shrine was of painted ceramic bricks. Even as he watched, a third brick slithered from its groove, and crashed on the pavement beneath.

Something must have started the bricks moving. Dekteon peered up. There was a flare of black wings. A large bird lifted from the roof, sailed across the orb of the moon. Dekteon blinked against the moon's whiteness, and the bird was gone.

A fourth brick crashed now, and others, falling more rapidly. Then the avalanche ended.

Dekteon returned through the garden to the small door. He could think of nothing else to do, though the night seemed alert now with unpredictable forces.

The door stood wide, as he had left it. He should not have left it like that. As he entered the door and pushed it shut behind him, and as the total dark of the passage closed over his eyes, Dekteon admitted that anyone, if they had wished, could have got in before him.

Dekteon paused.

It was ten paces to the angle of the wall, three more to gain the kitchen where the coals burned cheerfully. Just thirteen paces. That was all.

Dekteon took a step forward, another. Now he could no longer feel the door at his back, and he could glimpse nothing in front of him – or anywhere. A primaeval quickening washed over him. His heart began to race.

Without seeing or hearing it, without needing to touch or be touched by it, Dekteon knew, with complete certainty, that another presence was there with him, in the passage.

Never in all his life, never in his worst moment of panic, had Dekteon known such terror.

His reaction was headlong flight. He blundered into one wall and then into the other. No light appeared. There was an impression of space, and he sprawled forward over something. Sparks leapt behind his eyes. He realized the obstacle was the table. He had run into the kitchen area, but the coals were extinguished; he was as blind as in the passage.

Dekteon tried not to breathe. Now he was petrified, could not move. The awareness of a second presence was so awful, his brain seemed about to burst from his skull.

It gathered itself. All about him, gathered, tightened like a hand on his windpipe.

And then he heard something after all. It was a delicate noise, like tiny discs of thin beaten silver striking together.

Abruptly, the tension slackened. Dekteon felt the vice

let go of him, and he slumped again across the table. And as he did so, there formed upon the floor of the kitchen, in the darkness, one perfect silver footprint, and then, ahead of it, another, and another. As each came clear, that which had preceded it faded. There was no material shape. Nothing but these slender prints on the flagstones.

Accompanied by a tinkling of metal discs, the footprints went out of the kitchen. Impelled and reasonless, Dekteon staggered after. From below, he watched the insubstantial feet ascend the stairs to the spot where the wall of the tower bulged into the house. The footprints became static before the closed wooden door of the tower. On the door, a round red symbol appeared.

As the red symbol flamed, the print of the two feet dimmed, and suddenly went out, and terror withdrew as swiftly as it had come, like the passing of a cold, cold wind.

THREE

Zaister

At sun-up, White-Face emerged through the door of Zaister's tower. No symbol flared there now, but a little light was coming in at the south-eastern end of the hall. Dekteon had been sitting with his back to the bulging side of the tower. He could not recall settling himself there, nor much of the night, only that icy passing of fear, and the exhausted, semi-conscious vigil which followed it.

But a portion of Dekteon's brain and instinct had been waiting only for the opening of this door. Bemused, yet reacting instantly, he jumped up. He grabbed White-Face by the shoulder, pushed him against the wall and struck him across the head.

White-Face made no outcry and no protest, but his hood slid off. Again, Dekteon felt a dart of familiarity – which was impossible. For even in the poor light, he could see White-Face was utterly unlike anyone he had ever seen. The servant was entirely hairless. Not merely bald, but without eyebrows, lashes, or any hint of beard, shaven or otherwise. His colourless eyes were wide.

Prosaically he said, 'Did you watch?'

'Did I watch? Yes, I *watched*. Where's Zaister?'

'In the tower. Go up.'

Dekteon realized the mysterious tower door had been left open. Inside was a flight of narrow steps. Dekteon charged up them. He was angry, now fear had gone.

The steps wound upward and into a bare stone chamber. A long window faced east and Zaister stood before it. The sky in the window was ruddily golden, and the man's hair much the same colour. He did not turn, but he said, 'An unpleasant night perhaps? I'm sorry. But it had to be.'

'What?' Dekteon blurted.

'I'll tell you what. By day, they can only watch. But by night they're strong, and when the moon is full, they go hunting.'

Dekteon did not understand, yet the fear seemed to stir at Zaister's words.

'Some *thing*,' Dekteon said hoarsely. 'A noise like – like a girl's bracelet, and the print of *feet* . . .'

'Yes. There would be all of that. And more, maybe.'

'A black bird on the shrine roof. And a sheep in the yard.'

'Ah, the sheep. Be wary of them. They have the crescent on their backs.'

Dekteon took a breath. 'You aren't my lord. Today I'll be leaving.'

Zaister said, without malice, 'They've marked you now. Go where you want, they'd find you.'

Dekteon shuddered, cursing himself.

'Who are *they*?'

'The black-haired Daughters of Night,' Zaister said softly. 'The women, the moon's folk. While you, as I, are the red-haired man, Son of the Sun. Strong by day, vulnerable by night. Believe me.'

'This is some word-game. Lords play them, but not me. I'll be on my way. I'm no jest of yours.'

'Truly,' Zaister said, 'no game, no jest. Do you remember the hounds hunting you on the hill? That you did not like. But to be hunted, out in the open, by night, no shelter anywhere, hunted by the moon – there's no joy in that.'

Dekteon, bewildered and in blind fury, smashed his fist against the wall. He found he credited Zaister's words, without understanding a syllable of them.

'Be calm, my friend,' Zaister said. 'You've been put to use as the ox is put before the plough, which is very unfair. I owe you my reason, at least.'

Footsteps on the stair had Dekteon flinging himself aside frantically, but it was White-Face. Hooded once more, he bore a tray of beaten gold, and on it a flagon of gold and two gold cups for drinking. Despite the super-natural mood still on him, Dekteon was impressed. Even Fren had not possessed such riches.

White-Face set the gold things on the floor. He unstoppered the flagon and poured into the two cups. The liquid was the same hue as the gold. White-Face bore one cup to Zaister, one to Dekteon. Zaister drank, Dekteon hesitated. The drink was wine. He had smelled but never tasted wine before.

'Tell me, Dekteon,' Zaister said, 'what do you know of your world?' He spoke so casually, Dekteon tensed and did not answer. Zaister said, 'Not much, I should guess. A slave, uneducated, kept in the dark. But one thing you know, I think. You've had three masters. All men. And in your country, who rules?'

'A king,' Dekteon said slowly. 'In the highlands. The lords send him tribute.' He wanted to show Zaister he was not as ignorant as Zaister supposed.

'A king,' Zaister said. 'A man. And has the king a wife?'

'Three or four wives,' Dekteon said, pleased that he knew. 'That's the custom.'

'What would your opinion be,' said Zaister quietly, 'of a place where the king is a woman, who may take as many husbands as your king takes wives, and more?'

Dekteon laughed. This sounded like another joke, one that amused him this time.

Zaister smiled. 'You're lucky, my friend, to be able to laugh at it. You wouldn't laugh, I promise you, if you lived in such a country. A country where women are the masters. A country where the moon rules, and a man is simply the red sun-horse who draws the plough.'

'Is there such a place?'

'There is.'

'Where is it? I never heard tell of a land like this.'

'My poor slave, how much did you ever hear about the lands of the earth? But no, you couldn't, in any case, have learned of this one. It doesn't belong in your world.'

Dekteon stared.

Zaister drained his cup. He showed the cup to Dekteon.

'You look at this side of the cup, and cannot see the other. Yet you know the other side is there. Reverse the cup and you see the hidden side, but not the first side you looked at. And still you know the first side is present. Or again, if you look inside the cup you cannot see the outside of the cup. Or look at the outside and the inside is invisible. You follow me? Yes. Now the world which you inhabit is this side of the cup, and mine, this opposite side. Both exist but are hidden from each other. At least, in the general run of things they are. There are many worlds, many lands like this, existing side by side, end to end, each remote from each, yet close together as the sides of this cup. The sorcerer may find a way to travel them.'

Dekteon had taken a step backwards, without quite noticing he had. He understood, and did not understand. The harder he tried to grasp the words, the less he seemed able to. And yet, instinctively, *without* thinking, he did know exactly what Zaister meant.

Zaister was to be reckoned with. He knew facts about Dekteon which Dekteon had not mentioned, such as his three masters, the hounds Fren had set on him. Zaister had been expecting Dekteon in the wood and had sent his servant to fetch him. If anyone was a sorcerer, obviously Zaister was. Which, by what he said, meant he had travelled from another world into this. But what did Zaister really mean by 'world'? An unknown country, this was the nearest Dekteon could get. He was a slave. He could neither read nor write. No one had described the concept of the earth to him, it was just a word.

All his life, Dekteon had confronted lords who knew more than he did. Zaister was just another such

32

lord. Even so, Dekteon was nervous.

'What do you want me to do?' he said.

'Only listen for a minute, my friend,' Zaister said, 'and you shall learn. And drink your wine, you'll need it.'

Zaister reproached himself, even while he carried out his plan.

What he was doing was a callous, deplorable act. But then, if you were sufficiently afraid, sufficiently desperate, you would do anything. Then again, if he had ever been taught any pride in his manhood, as were the men in this ridiculous and primitive world, perhaps he might have been different. But where he came from it was the women who were proud, and strong. And cruel. And terrifyingly relentless.

He thought of the silver feet poised before the door of the tower, which only the sorcerous red sun-brand had kept at bay. A whole year they had been gathering now, to break through to him in this precarious haven he had won for himself. Each night of full moon they had been a little more powerful.

Zaister began to tell Dekteon about his life. He wondered how much Dekteon took in. Doubtless not much. But Zaister felt compelled to speak, to explain.

Zaister talked of the rich landscape of his world, the colours, which made Dekteon's world, by comparison, drab and monochrome. Zaister spoke of a huge city, with towers that seemed built of green fire, where white lionesses walked at the heels of the women, obedient as dogs were to the men of earth. Zaister spoke of the woman-king, and when he did so, his voice broke. Izvire the Moon, Daughter of Night, Lord of the City. His wife.

That was, his wife for five years. After which, the woman-king took a new consort.

The husband of the woman-king, the moon's partner, represented the sun. Accordingly, he was not permitted to grow old. If he did, the sun might also fail, the lands be blighted and the mountains topple. It was an old religion. Despite the magic certain of the people of Zaister's world had come to know and to utilise, they still adhered to these beliefs. The sun consort must be a red-haired man and well-favoured. For five years he would be the companion of the woman-king. He would give her children. He would be honoured. Next to his wife he would be the highest in the city and the kingdom. But at the five years' end, there would be a new consort, in order that the sun remain ever young and vital. The former consort, no longer the sun, would be invested with the sins of the people. He would be made a scapegoat. He would be slain.

Zaister told himself, if he had been called on to die in some other fashion, for some other reason, it might have been different. In a battle perhaps, fighting to preserve the city – he did not imagine he would have shirked that. He was not a coward. But this. And it was not even – not even a *good* death . . .

But he was not going to hide from himself in words. He had been afraid when the fourth year ended and the last year of his term began. He had fallen to thinking of his death, and of his sorcery, and presently he had used that sorcery and fled. Out of his world, to Dekteon's, or as near it as he was able to get. For, despite what he had said, it was not quite possible to transfer himself totally, as he was, from his own environ to another. This place was not on his world, nor on Dekteon's, but somewhere between the two. It had characteristics and borrowings of both, yet its very appearance gave it away as something not entirely feasible. What was real here, and what was phantom? Zaister was not sure himself. He had assembled the mansion, but it evolved as a ruin for he lacked the knowledge to construct better. And day by day it became more ruinous, less substantial, while now and then elements from the real worlds intruded. And, as the Daughters of Night came closer in their pursuit, intruded more often.

It had taken Zaister, having found Dekteon, almost the whole year to prepare and entrap him. And during that year Zaister knew that gradually the Moon Priestesses, the Daughters of Night, were eroding his magic. At first, their attempts had been feeble and negligent. But as Zaister's last year as consort drew towards its end, the women grew more dangerous and more determined. At full moon last night they had got very near. Only Dekteon's presence here had counteracted and diverted their spells. Next full moon marked the end of Zaister's term. That night Zaister was meant to die. And he had no doubt the priestesses would succeed in reaching him, and in slaying him in the prescribed manner.

Except that now Dekteon would intervene.

It was curious for Zaister to remember that Dekteon, untutored slave that he was, was really *himself*. For

Dekteon *was* Zaister, Zaister as he would have been, had he been born on this parallel yet dissimilar earth. As there were two like sides to the cup, and two approximate worlds, so there were counterparts among the people of these worlds.

It had been quite easy to trace his counterpart. Dekteon even looked very like him, somewhat darker, a little younger, but virtually the same. And being ignorant as he was, Dekteon had been extremely suggestible.

Dekteon had never wondered about the old slave in the Shore House at By-the-Lake. Yet the old slave's constant warnings had actually pushed Dekteon, contrary and hot-headed as he was, into the stupidity and bravado that finally earned him a sentence to the copper mines. And then the old slave had cut his bonds, instructed him to flee to the ring of standing stones . . . Dekteon had taken the old slave's advice. If he had noticed something odd about the standing stones, he did not falter. Zaister's sorcery had set them there only hours before, as he had set the old slave – who was nothing of the sort – in Fren's household. Just as the 'slave' had looked old, so did the stones. Neither was a mortal thing, and so could be projected fully into Dekteon's world, as Zaister, ironically, could not project himself, being otherworld flesh.

The central slab of the stone ring bore certain runes. They suggested to Dekteon's unconscious mind that he raise the stone and hide beneath. Under it lay a Vortex which presently propelled Dekteon from his own world to this intermediary one.

It was an essential of the sorcery that Dekteon came

willingly, or so Zaister's researches had told him. Hence the elaborateness of the plans. But now, at last, there was no need for lies.

Zaister regarded Dekteon with pity and remorse, yet quite implacably.

Zaister's only means of escape from death was on to Dekteon's dreary earth and into Dekteon's role of hunted slave. Still, Zaister would carry his learning and cleverness with him, just as poor Dekteon would carry his own ignorance and bewilderment into Zaister's life – what was left of it.

The vengeful power of the Daughters had already marked Dekteon. Now he could be sent in Zaister's place, to be dragged to die in Zaister's stead. And Zaister would go free.

'I'm sorry,' Zaister said, as before, 'sincerely. I regret condemning you to this. But I want my life. And I mean to have it.'

As Zaister had surmised, Dekteon did not assimilate very much of what he had been told. It sounded like gibberish. Another world – a land of women who were kings. That Zaister must die, yet somehow Dekteon could be made to die instead.

'Did you drink your wine?' Zaister asked. He crossed to Dekteon, and looked in the golden cup. It was empty. Dekteon had drunk, probably without being aware of doing so. That was excellent. The wine contained various ingredients which would aid Zaister's sorcery, as the food and drink had done previously.

Dekteon looked at Zaister narrowly. Perhaps Zaister

was mad? Dekteon had felt an impulse to serve him, a foolish impulse. Only the servant stood between Dekteon and the doorway. The door to the tower had not been shut.

Dekteon moved suddenly. He flung the golden cup in Zaister's face, and spinning about, thrust the servant from his path.

Dekteon ran through the doorway, on to the stair and down it. He plunged through the open tower door, across the Hall and into the courtyard of the house.

Above the avenue of lions and dogs, the sky was bright lavender, more like dusk than early morning. The walls and the three south-east towers rose jaggedly against it. The towers seemed higher. On the top of each was a rosy glowing bloom, like fiery smoke, but static. Dekteon blinked, but the bloom did not go.

As he stared about, the cart horse came into view. It was standing beside the well with the tree growing from it. Neither the tree nor the horse were the same. The tree was a hard shining white, without leaves; the horse seemed to stand taller on its bear's feet. Two straight pointed horns sheared back from the ridges over its eyes.

Dekteon no longer attempted to reason this magic out. He had hesitated, now he began to run again. He raced for the gate, and the open valley beyond.

Strangely, no one followed him.

FOUR

Sorcery by Day and Night

His intention was simple. He did not need to explain it to himself. Despite all Zaister's words, Dekteon was still thinking in terms of his own world. He had not understood Zaister, or had not wanted to.

Dekteon was making for the valley's edge, and then for the woods where he had woken, and which had taken so many hours of journeying in the servant's cart. To judge from the positions of the sun, which Dekteon had been able to perceive even through the mist as they travelled, he had been brought in a northerly direction to the valley. Besides, there had been the paved track the cart had used, which should be easy to stay with. Once he had reached the woods, Dekteon had a hope of discovering the river, whether he had crossed it or not. He could not have got far from the circle of stones that day, in his fever.

No, he did not believe Zaister. Zaister was clever, a magician maybe, trying to scare Dekteon. He could create illusions – the horned horse, for example.

Dekteon ran.

He had no thought of Fren, or Fren's search-party with its dogs. If he had stopped to consider, Dekteon would have seen that his lack of anxiety about Fren meant that, inside himself, he did believe Zaister after all.

Below the earthworks, he avoided running on the open track, only keeping by it, to the side, among the shells of the stone houses. There was no sign of the wild sheep. The sky was clear of bird or cloud. The houses looked normal; tumbled roofs, mossy steps. Yet, when Dekteon glanced over his shoulder, he thought for a split second there was a range of intact glittering buildings marching across the valley. Then they were gone.

It had needed less than half of an hour for the cart to cross the valley. It seemed to be taking Dekteon much longer. His muscles and lungs were sound, he could keep at racing speed a good while. Yet somehow the upward south-eastern incline for which he was heading apparently got no nearer.

The trees which clad the lower slopes that led from the valley were a fierce ripe red. The grass had lost its soft wintery tinge. It was like green peppermint.

Abruptly, running between the houses, Dekteon found himself on a street. Bits of paving were still sunk in the earth. The houses closed in on either hand, shutting out the line of the other track. Dekteon stopped running. He walked along the street. At its end it broadened into a square which was laid with rectangular smooth stones, and at its centre stood a marble basin with clear water gushing up from a spout.

Beyond the basin, Dekteon could see the south-east slope rising from the valley, but all around, the houses closed him in. The water splashed with a crystalline noise. It made him unbearably thirsty.

Dekteon went to the basin, cupping his hands to trap the water. As he leaned over it, the water disappeared.

The marble basin was overgrown with weeds and the spout choked with them. The water had dried up years ago. Yet he had heard it, seen it – almost tasted it.

Dekteon turned away, and at once he heard the water again, bubbling from the spout. Dekteon looked back. It was no longer water, but wine. Dekteon put out his hand. He thrust his fingers against the spout, and the wine spilled over them. But when he put the fingers to his mouth, they were dry.

Dekteon left the fountain, which must be another of Zaister's tricks, and walked back up the street, between the ruined houses. When he came to the part of the street which crumbled off into the grass, he was confronted instead by a tall stone wall that had not been there before, or had not seemed to be. The wall appeared real enough, and presently Dekteon began to climb up it, using the rough subsiding stones as handholds.

He reached the top of the wall without difficulty, but on the other side he saw another square, like the first, and another marble basin in it, and water sparkling. Dekteon was not afraid. He felt only a sort of numbness. He sat on the wall, looking at the basin and the water.

The sun was warm on his back. It was rising to the noon zenith. Rising too quickly, Dekteon thought. Only a couple of hours had passed, perhaps a little more, since sunrise. But then, somehow Zaister was detaining him in the valley, and probably Dekteon had been here, running in circles, for longer than he recalled. He should have been alarmed at this, but was not. The warmth of the sun, the gentle pleasant sound of the undrinkable magic water relaxed him.

Some rabbits were playing about at the edge of the square: black rabbits, two or three of them. A solitary bird floated lazily across the sky.

Dekteon shut his eyes. He was able to ignore his thirst.

He forgot about Zaister.

When he woke it was bitterly cold. A raw wind was blowing, thrashing red leaves before it through the overgrown street.

Dekteon was appalled. The sky had become overcast, and the sun swam through patches of darkness, but obviously it was past the zenith now. The wall he had climbed was only a foot or so high, and the basin in the square was nothing of the sort, but an old brick well furred with lichen. Dekteon abandoned the wall and pushed through a tangle of briars. The original track that led from Zaister's mansion was about ten yards away. This time Dekteon did not hesitate to follow it. Clearly no one bothered with chasing him. The valley itself was brimful of snares and sorceries. It seemed to him he had only his instinct to counter them. His instinct said: 'Be fearful, trust nothing.'

He was thankful for the cold which had roused him. He started to run once more. He stared at the slope ahead. On this occasion he would reach it.

Half an hour later, keeping to the track, he was on the incline that led from the valley.

He had lessened his sprint to a steady jogging, the pace he had learned when he had had to carry messages for his former masters across the length and breadth of their estates. He did not feel the cold any more. His blood sang. The trees on the slope had lost some of their unnatural red colour. He jogged into them and emerged above them. The paved track spread up and over the crest of the slope, as he remembered. The mist had faded there on his arrival, just in time to reveal the valley, having hidden so much of the journey before. There was no mist now, however, only the ragged sky blowing over above.

At the top of the track, Dekteon paused, turned round and gaped at the valley. He was not sure why he did this, perhaps to check there was no pursuit.

Nothing stirred below, except for the trees ruffled by the wind. He could see shadows of clouds reflected on the plain as they rushed by. Then he made out another cloud-shadow that was not moving quite in line with the rest, as it veered slowly between the ruined houses. It was the flock of wild sheep. He had not encountered them as he crossed the plain, but now they were slowly eddying along in much the same direction as he had taken, out on to the paved track.

He recollected the single sheep in the courtyard. He recollected, too, what Zaister had said: '. . . the sheep. Be wary of them. They have the crescent on their backs.'

Dekteon moved on and began his jogging pace once

more. He was out of the valley. Now he must get through the woods and locate the river. Sheep were unimportant.

Something darted across Dekteon's path.

Instinctively he swerved to avoid it. Doubtless it was some woodland creature he had disturbed, flying for cover in alarm. But then the thing, or another just like it, dashed out again, almost under his feet.

The third time it happened, he glimpsed what it was. A black rabbit. No, three black rabbits.

Dekteon increased his speed. He ran fast but the rabbits kept up with him. Every second or so, one or other of them would fling itself across his tracks. It was like an unnatural game.

A rabbit pelted diagonally between his feet. He felt the small hard impact of its body. His left foot turned. He barely prevented himself falling, and brought himself to a staggering halt.

The rabbit lay not far from him on the bright leaves; it was twitching, its eyes like frosty glass. It had been hurt by this collision with a running man, and his impulse was to go and put it out of its pain. But somehow he went no closer.

A delicate pattering among the nearest trees told him the other rabbits were still there. If he ran on, they would begin again to hound him. Black rabbits, black sheep, black birds – the things of night . . . Zaister's lesson was coming home to Dekteon.

The rabbit lying on the leaves suddenly flopped on its belly and then dragged itself up. Its eyes focussed, and it stared at him.

The wood seemed to be darkening as if a storm were brewing.

The rabbit raised itself to its hind limbs. There was something uncanny about it. The long claws in its forefeet were unsheathed.

Deliberately, Dekteon turned away from it, and began to walk, not run, along the track.

Soon he heard little precise sounds behind him, but nothing darted or tried to impede his progress.

Above, the storm was thickening, but the sun was still visible, westering now. He had an hour of daylight left, which was illogical – the day had lasted merely four or five hours. Or less. And when night closed down on him, then what? The things of night had marked him, and the women of Zaister's land, or world, were intent on vengeance.

Yes, Dekteon was afraid. But not really afraid in the right way. It was a lethargic leaden fear, that slowed him rather than spurred him to flight.

In a stand of leaning trees, the paved track ended.

This entire portion of the journey to the valley had been shrouded in mist, and in sleep, for he had slept then, too, in the cart of Zaister's servant. Now all Dekteon knew, or thought he knew, was that he must continue to head south. Walking, with an escort of three rabbits scuttling behind.

The storm did not break. The western sky reddened and the east darkened further. The wind dropped.

Long shadows rayed from the trees.

He could not reach the wood before sundown, and he would not reach the river. Dekteon was hungry. He had not eaten since that meal given him yesterday in the kitchen of Zaister's mansion.

It came to Dekteon without warning that he did believe what Zaister had told him. Danger was all about, and no escape from it. Nor was there any destination, such as a river or an outlaw camp, which might harbour him. Wherever he was, this place of abbreviated days, mists, sinister beasts, this place was not the earth he had been born to.

Walk or run as swift as he might, he could not now outdistance this awareness.

Dekteon had crested a low hill. He could stare down to the south. A fading red cloud on the horizon might be the woodland. Or might not.

Patter-patter on leaves behind him.

Southward, the sky seemed to curve upwards in an absurd concave fashion, like the sides of a bowl. Perhaps that was what it was. A bowl of sky containing Zaister's makeshift place between the worlds.

Dekteon crouched down and let his head hang forwards, like a weary dog. He was worn out. He was literally at his wits' end. He thought: If I had been trained, if I were cunning, like a priest or a mage . . . But he wondered what they would do, actually, snarled in this frightening lunacy.

The final stages of light were sinking from the sky. When would the moon rise? What forces would rise with it?

A black flicker moved along the ground nearby: the three rabbits. Dekteon had killed a rabbit once, in Fren's forest, broken its neck and taken the carcase to be cooked by the slaves in secret. There had not been enough to eat that winter, though Fren's table was piled high. Fren never found out about the poaching. The rabbit had been very easy to catch and to kill. Dekteon had even pitied it.

But these rabbits were not the same. Their heads were long and lean. They sat in trio, almost comical, yet somehow not. And as the light died, their eyes began to glimmer.

Dekteon crouched, watching the rabbits as they watched him.

Night absorbed sky and land. For miles not a sound, not a lamp. Of course there would be no lamps. Only three men moved about in this place. Zaister, Zaister's servant, Dekteon.

After a while Dekteon got up and began to walk on, down the hill, southward, aimlessly. And the rabbits bobbed tirelessly behind him.

The sheep were galloping from the north. There were fifty of them, or eighty, or a hundred. Their small feet gave off a brisk clatter on the track, and later a sullen thunder on the grassy soil.

Like a herd of horses, the sheep ran. Black as molasses, they poured up slopes and boiled over the tops and spilled down the other sides. Their eyes were like beads of polished resin, one hundred beads or one hundred and sixty or two hundred beads, each bead gleaming in the dark.

About half a mile behind the sheep, but moving in the same direction, a figure came at a tireless fast lope.

The eyes of the figure also shone. He was totally hairless, and as he sped across the ground he held his arms outstretched before him, as if to balance.

Eastwards, the moon was rising, no longer full, an imperfect disc.

Dekteon was in a ravine when the moon rose. Almost simultaneously, he heard the strange dull thunder behind him. He turned, and saw a darkness swirl over the slope.

Compulsively, Dekteon began to run.

It must be dogs behind him, dogs after his scent. They would tear him in pieces, as the hounds of Fren would have done.

Three bits of mobile blackness shot past Dekteon, and away to the left, eastward. The rabbits, leaving him, anxious to avoid the dogs, no doubt.

Whose dogs were they? Zaister's?

Virtually the moment he started to run, Dekteon started also to flag. He would not get far. The drum of pursuit seemed to pound inside his head.

The land began to rise once more. Trees thrust from the uneven ground, slowing him further.

Dekteon stumbled. A tree offered him sinuous arms – he fell against it and the arms seemed to grapple him. Dekteon beat the branches aside. They slashed at his hands and face and his fine red clothes, and his hair. The injured skin of his back which since the mysterious salve had been applied to it had not hurt him, now began to burn like fires. A twig tore across his cheek, barely missing his eye. The tree was apparently alive, and determined to restrain him.

Dekteon became conscious of silence beyond the noise of his struggle, and ceased struggling to squint between the claws of the tree. He made out a pack of animals, stone-still in the light of the moon.

The hounds had reached him, and had no need to hurry now. But he could see they were not dogs. It was the mob of wild sheep which had chased him.

They stood pressed close together. Their eyes shone, each one with its crescent of white moonlight.

The tree released Dekteon, if it had really held him. Perhaps only his panic had made it appear to do so. Brittle branches snapped off, and showered about his feet.

The sheep were everywhere around him. Very leisurely, one mincing step at a time, they began to move inwards.

They were larger than he had estimated. Their faces had all the bland complaisance of sheep, yet no vacancy. They were intent, intelligent.

Transfixed, Dekteon thought: What can they do to me? The weight of their bodies, perhaps, would be used to push him off balance. Then they could trample over him. Well, he must keep upright. But he had no resource left to meet this gruesome silly challenge.

One of the sheep was ahead of the rest. It was a ram; he had not seen it before. Two huge milky horns curled down on either side of its head, curved horns which were like the crescent moon. The ram suddenly flung up its head, wrinkling its upper lip, and Dekteon got a sight of its teeth. They were not, after all, the mild square teeth of a herbivore. Each one was narrow and sharply pointed: the carnivorous fangs of a beast that preyed on flesh.

At this moment a figure erupted over the brow of the hill, its arms outstretched before it, dead white in the moon with a white skull of a head; Zaister's hairless servant.

Horrified, Dekteon did not puzzle at this new figment of the nightmare. But the sheep unaccountably hesitated in their menacing advance.

As White-Face plunged against the barrier of sheep, Dekteon expected them to round on him and rip him with their fangs, but instead they trotted aside and let him through.

White-Face stopped running and lowered his arms. Something odd was happening to him. He bent forward, he seemed to shrivel and dry out. His skin darkened and crinkled. Thin hair formed like smoke on his head. He wore the wretched patchwork clothes of a slave, and lifting his hand, he pointed at Dekteon in a way Dekteon remembered.

'They think you're too weak to get away now, and you are,' Fren's old slave said to him, 'but you must try. Follow the uplands,' Fren's old slave said, 'there is a ring of stones.'

Dekteon began to shiver and could not control the shivering. He gazed past the familiar figure of the old slave – the old slave who had irritated and warned and finally rescued him in Fren's house, the old slave who, all the while, had been Zaister's pale servant – and gazed northward, up the hill, at the ring of ancient stones which now inexorably leaned there as if they had done so for centuries.

'Come,' the old slave said precisely. 'You are stayed for.'

Dekteon's limbs felt hollow, without muscle or blood in them, but somehow they carried him, through the avenue between the sheep, back up the hill the way he had come, into the ring of stones.

At the ring's centre was a black pit. Unable to resist, or argue, or cry aloud, Dekteon jumped into the pit.

The night sprang forward with Dekteon clamped in its jaws.

Part Two

Part Two

FIVE

The Women

The women rode down from the hill.

There were five of them. They wore black garments, heavily fringed with silver; their black breeches were embroidered with silver thread and silver girdles bound each of their narrow waists. Their boots were of white cow hide, and the bows slung over their shoulders of layered white ivory. They were mounted on lions which were reddish in colour with blood-red manes. Short horns grew straight up from the foreheads of the lions.

The moon, almost full though waning, shone behind the women as they came down from the hill to where the man lay.

One of the women dismounted. She stood over the man. Her black hair poured round her white face.

'Lord Zaister,' she said flatly, 'welcome, Sun's Son, on your return.'

The man opened his eyes. He wore scarlet garments edged with yellow, a collar of gold. His hair was a light golden-red. His look was one of puzzlement, then of fear. He said:

'I'm not Zaister.'

The woman scornfully smiled. 'Oh, no, lord. If you say you're not. By what name shall we call the Sun's Son?' She glanced back at the other women. 'Lord Zaister wishes to change his name now he's home.'

The other women grinned, all but one. She was not like the four she rode with, who were young. This woman was old, her hair a dark metallic grey, her body thin and raddled, yet upright on her lion-mount. She rode the beast forward.

'The lord is Zaister, and may not change his name to please himself,' she said. Her voice was harsh as a crow's cawing. To match it, the man now saw, she had a crow perched upon her saddle, still as could be, all but its fierce eyes. The old woman's eyes were filmed over; she seemed blind. Without warning, she bent sideways from her saddle, and seized the man's face in her bony hand. 'Yes, this is he,' she said, 'come reluctantly back to us. Are you ready to die now, lord? In a month's time, as you must?'

The other woman frowned.

'We never speak of the Last Month, Kyrast,' she said.

'Don't we, lass? *I* do.'

The man flinched away from the old woman called Kyrast.

'My name is Dekteon,' he said. He shivered.

The old woman released him. She seemed to be considering what he had said. Her filmed eyes made her look as if she were staring inwards. But she only stroked the crow with her finger, and directed her strange mount a little way back up the hill without another word.

The man, who truly was Dekteon, said, 'Zaister was a sorcerer. He left your – your land, and came to another. I met him there. He tried to make me serve him.'

The standing woman laughed at that, a cold hard bark. None of the women were like any he had seen before: arrogant and proud and – what was it? Undaunted. They carried themselves like lords and princes. Even Fren's First Wife had not carried herself like this.

'Sun's Son,' the woman said, 'we know you used magic arts to hide for a year, and we could not immediately reach you, despite our anxieties for your well-being. Such an act is displeasing to our goddess the Moon, and to the god of the Sun, whose child you are. You must answer for that act. And it's no answer, lord, to say you're another, when plainly you are yourself.'

Behind her, the old woman called out:

'Show him his likeness, girl.'

The woman went on, with her smile, 'Yes, he would take delight in that. Lord Zaister was always entertained to see his own beauty. Look then, Sun's Son.'

There was a silver thing hanging at her belt. She raised it and light flashed off and he realized it was a round silver mirror. She held the mirror near him, so he could observe himself reflected there.

Dekteon gazed, then seized the looking glass so roughly the woman mocked him. What Dekteon saw gazing back at him was the horrified face of Zaister, wreathed by Zaister's hair.

The women of Dekteon's world were not like these women. They did not have this peculiar tone and bearing. Nor did they have daggers at their belts and bows on their backs and ride horned lions.

The old woman, Kyrast, had a collar and armlets of silver with white gems set in them. She rode slightly ahead of the rest, easy yet imperious on her loping beast. She seemed to be the captain of this group, and the other woman, who had shown him the mirror, was her lieutenant.

From a shadowy grove at the top of the hill, they had produced a horse for Dekteon. It was a red horse with bear's feet; its bridle was beaded, but the bridles of the women were plain. Straight horns grew from its brow ridges.

Dekteon tried to master his continuing fear.

Even by night, under the harshness of the moon, he could see this country was not his own, nor any he had ever heard of. Moment by moment fresh bizarre details intruded on his senses.

The slopes and hills about were carpeted by a velvet weed or moss quite unlike grass. The trees which rose solitary or in groves were unbelievably slim and tall, lifting a hundred feet or more into the air, but without lower branches. At their tops they burst into foliage that glowed in the moonlight like plumes of incandescent gas. He could not tell their colour by night. Yet in the far distance was something whose colour he could tell, a rich iridescence on the eastern horizon. Dekteon had no notion what it could be. It looked like a huge fire. A huge *dark green* fire, from which smokes of other shades were drifting.

There were stars in this sky but their patterns were

unfamiliar. Even the smell of this land was alien.

He went with the women because they expected it and he was too distraught to argue. He guessed at what Zaister had done. In some illogical sorcerous way Zaister had given Dekteon his own – Zaister's – image. At least, a good enough replica to fool these women, who took him for the husband of their woman-king, and meant to kill him when the month ended.

Presumably, it was to the king they were conducting him, to 'answer' for his 'unpleasing act' – Zaister's withdrawal into hiding.

Dekteon became aware then that his fear was somehow drifting away of its own accord, leaving him simply surprised. All this was impossible. None of it could be happening. Would he meet death with surprise, too? Dekteon's mind, which had borne already too much, shouldered this off. He had a month. Till next full moon, wasn't it? Yes, that must be it. There would be a way to escape. They were only women. Women did not kill men merely to ensure sunrise. Women were dependent on men for their strength, for security and for children.

They rode over the hill and down the other side. Dekteon began to notice similarities to the country which had surrounded the ruin in the valley, the placing of things rather than their appearance. He came to anticipate an equivalent to the paved track, and sure enough there was. Although this one was raised three feet from the terrain about it, a causeway. The paving blocks were regular, of pure white marble. Trees had been planted on either side at exact intervals. These were unlike the tall branchless trees, being squat and cone shaped. If it was autumn here, Dekteon could not be sure. No leaves fell.

The women were silent. Their grim, finely-moulded features gave away too much of their contempt. He wondered how the old woman saw with her blinded eyes. Probably the lion-steed knew the way. Once, she let the crow fly. It soared up in the air and wheeled about and then returned. Its wings were broader than crow's wings generally are. Dekteon recalled the black bird which had pushed the tiles from the shrine roof at the ruined mansion.

The unnatural fire on the horizon went on burning. At length, the sky there began to lighten further. It became crimson, then pale red, then gold. It was the dawn. A very swift and savage dawn. Red clouds raced out of the sunrise into the remaining darkness overhead which was altered to indigo. The other fire on the horizon seemed to dim and sink. Then the sun came up on long extended rays, an amber disc that was clearly visible, for it was not as bright as the sun of Dekteon's world. Able to study it unblinking, his mouth went dry, though his fear was gone.

All around, the land ignited into colours, dazzling him.

He noticed the women.

Until then they had treated him with an off-hand authoritarianism. Now they had reined in their mounts, swung down from the saddles, and clustered about him, their eyes bright.

'Blessed be the Sun's Son,' Kyrast's lieutenant said. Her voice was friendly, almost affectionate. 'We are rejoiced that you are with us once more, lord.' And she bowed to him, and the other three bowed also. Only the old one took no notice, uninterested.

Dekteon said, 'I'm not Zaister.'

The lieutenant took his hand and pressed her brow to it. 'Then tell us, lord, which name you wish us to give you.'

'Dekteon,' he said. He felt foolish, yet somehow relaxed, pleased. He did not elaborate, or again protest.

He had been given the body of another man. Perhaps that other man would have responded in this way. Was it a part of the magic that now he would grow not only to resemble, but to *be* Zaister? A pampered, spoiled Zaister, who went, unresisting, to die.

'Dekteon,' the women said.

They laughed, not in the cold way of before. They laughed as if they were happy to do what would please him. Like a fond mother with a baby . . . The sun had risen, that was why they had changed to him. Day was the man's time. Night, the woman's. He knew this. Zaister had told him, but no, not only because Zaister had told him. Zaister's body and brain, now his, understood these customs.

They went on, but more slowly. The lieutenant woman walked, and led his horse, her own lion following her obediently.

It was a beautiful morning, stunningly so. The sky was lilac. The leaves of the shorter trees were brazen, the tall trees a gaseous rose. Eastward, extraordinary bands like rainbows ran across the slopes, which, as they began to ride through them, he found to be pastures,

61

close-packed with flowers, blue, violet, yellow, purple and cream. The causeway went over a lavender canal. A man walked by through the flower-fields with a herd of large cat-like animals – a shepherd of tigers?

In the east, a tourmaline city of a thousand towers started to form on the horizon.

The city occupied a valley and several hills. Dekteon had never seen or heard of a city so enormous. Its faceted green buildings gleamed and glittered.

Birds were flying over it as they came near. Here and there blue-pink smokes went up from mysterious vents.

It was like something from a dream.

The mood of the women had softened further as they rode towards it. One had made flower chaplets and roped them round the horns of Dekteon's horse. The lieutenant mounted her lion and joined Kyrast at the front of their little procession. Two others placed themselves each side of him; the last woman brought up the rear. He realized it was a guard, but whether for an honoured prince or a captured prisoner he was not sure.

The gates of the city were at least eighty feet high. They stood open.

There were people about, near the gates and inside, coming and going. He saw women, and men, but more of the former. Both sexes were dressed much alike, tunics cut diagonally across the hip to allow free movement, breeches and boots. Both wore their hair long. He spotted no red-headed men, and no black-haired men either. On the other hand, the women were all strikingly jet-black of hair. Perhaps it was dyed to conformity.

There also seemed to be a colour taboo. The men wore various shades of brown and blue, occasionally a raucous orange or wealthy purple. The women wore only black. It made them seem ominous. Black garments, black hair, white faces and hands. Daughters of Night. Yes, the title was apt.

There was another, less obvious, singularity. The men did not stride about their business. It was the women who did that. Coming face to face, it was the man who gave the woman right of way.

A woman in an iron chariot swirled down the track that led to the gate. Three white tigers galloped in the shafts.

Though he noticed manual labourers in the city, servants, even warrior-guards – and all of them men – none of them had the presence that the women had.

But events had taken a turn now that made Dekteon himself a focus of interest. No sooner were they in the gate, than twenty men came trotting up on the bear-horses. Apparently these were the warriors of the city. They had brazen helmets, chest-pieces and greaves; swords hung on either side of their belts, and they had spears in their hands. They saluted the five women, in particular Kyrast. They formed up about the party.

The crowd was already leaving off its activity to stare. Gradually a humming noise began which presently swelled into a stupendous roar.

For a minute, Dekteon took the noise for anger. He had heard little else all his life as a slave. Yet the great roar went on and on, and flowers rained over him, and he understood it was a welcome. More, a cry of passionate adulation.

Dekteon's heart unaccountably lifted. The cry seemed to strengthen him. It should not have done. They were crying for their five-year Sun, soon to go down in blood, for the scapegoat of their sins. Yet the noise thrilled Dekteon. Not Zaister's reaction at all. But then, Zaister had never been a slave, cursed and beaten and hounded. Zaister had been adored since his birth, for his hair had marked him from the first for religious honour and rank.

The wide marble road led on, and upwards. Dekteon made out a high wall at the end of it, and gardens rising from behind the wall. The trees, there, seemed to be in white blossom. At the summit of the gardens was a precipice of green building. But the roofs of the building were white as the trees, and sickle-horned, like the moon.

He glanced at the woman riding by him. It was the one who had garlanded his horse with flowers.

'What house is that?'

The woman beamed at him.

'Lord Zaister jokes with me.'

'I told you, I'm not Zaister.'

'Oh, yes. I see. Very well, lord.' She was prepared to play the game with him, keep the child amused. 'It is the Moon Palace.'

'Are we going there?'

'Oh, *yes*, lord.'

'Why?'

'To meet your wife, lord. Izvire, the Moon.'

'Your king.'

'*The* king.'

Dekteon felt a renewed twinge of nervousness. Not actual fear, but almost embarrassment. Zaister's wife.

'Did Zaister live in her palace?'

The woman, plainly taken with the jest, giggled. And for a moment Dekteon caught sight of a real woman behind her face.

'Er, *Zaister*, Sun's Son – he lives in the brother palace, the Sun's House.'

'Where is the Sun's House?'

'To the right, lord. That hill, you can see it now, between the roofs.'

The hill was surmounted by yet more walls, but golden discs there flashed back early sunlight. Gold for the Sun's Son, silver for the Moon's Daughter.

'Why aren't you taking me there?'

'Izvire has not seen her husband for almost a year, lord.'

'And time's short,' said Dekteon bitterly. Yet he was exhilarated. 'Tell me, when he's dead, does she hang the flayed skin of him on the wall?'

The woman was shocked for a moment. He had offended her stupid hag's religion.

The streak of inbred, frustrated rebellion that had always been there in Dekteon, flared up. He had stolen and poached and ridden his master's horses in one world. Now he stood in his stirrups and, ignoring the warrior guard, the crowds, the women, ignoring most of all his weird plight, he yelled:

'Kyrast! Hey, old lady – is Zaister's wife as old as you? How many husband-skins has she got on her wall?'

65

And Kyrast veered round stiffly in her saddle to stare back at him through the cataracts in her eyes.

A wild triumph shot across Dekteon's body. In his world he had had no chance. Mutiny was always smashed there. But here they would not harm him, not quite yet. Because he was the sacred consort.

He could do anything, and no one would whip him, beat him, brand him, set dogs on him.

He had a whole month of utter freedom. And then he would find some way to elude them. Run, if he had to, as before. This world seemed as large as his own, and larger.

Dekteon looked at the girl riding by him.

'I don't want this king of yours,' he said. 'You be my wife. All you women look the same, but you're pretty enough.'

And the girl flushed angrily, like any girl of his own world, suddenly unsure of herself.

Dekteon began to whistle the slave song he had remembered on the battlements of Zaister's ruin, in the mist.

The moon walks east of midnight,
The sun walks west of noon.

It was applicable, he thought. All around, the crowd gaped. The old woman rode with her stiff spine stiffer. The girl chewed her lip.

And though I love you, sweetheart,
I will not sing your tune.

Nor yours, Izvire, he thought. Whatever it is.

SIX

Izvire

He did not know her, had never seen her, yet already he felt things about her. Probably because of the situation. Probably because this replica of Zaister's body remembered her, somehow. The memories were vague, and mixed, strife, envy, fear, admiration, love, all had a say in them.

Dekteon had known several girls. A couple of them he had liked, though slave-life did not lend itself to permanence. In his experience, he had never felt any of these things for a woman that Zaister had felt for his.

Dekteon's nervousness, nevertheless, returned. He swaggered more to keep it at bay.

The garden was white. White flowers underfoot, white-flowered trees above against the mauve sky. The inner rooms of the palace were also white. The old woman and her four female soldiers led him upstairs, downstairs, finally into a hall. There was no fireplace. Instead, green and blue chemical fires burned in braziers.

Izvire – he assumed it was she – sat on an ivory chair, waiting for him. He was disappointed. She wore white, not black, and a silver moon-mask, with slanting eyes and a slit for a mouth, was clapped on her face to hide it. But otherwise she looked just like the rest, slim and pale, with long black hair. He was positive when she removed the mask he would hardly be able to tell her from the others.

Kyrast snapped her fingers at the female escort.

'Out!'

They went at once. The warriors had halted at the palace door.

'Well, so you are home again, Sun's Son,' the woman in the mask said. The voice was cold. The mask turned to Kyrast. 'He forgets himself, my Zaister.'

Kyrast walked slowly to a table. Slowly she poured wine for herself from a silver ewer. She must be able to see somewhat, after all.

'He says, Izvire, that he isn't Zaister.'

'No doubt. A great jester is my husband.'

Then Izvire the Moon got up. The instant she moved, Dekteon heard a sound that made his hair stir on his neck; the delicate tinkling of tiny discs of beaten silver striking together. Just as he had heard it that night in the pitch-black passage when terror took him by the throat. Involuntarily, his eyes went to her feet. She wore satin shoes, and left no footprint on the floor. Her bracelets, three on each wrist, made the tinkling sound.

'Ah,' she said, 'he recollects *that*, Kyrast. Don't be afraid, Zaister. You've come back to fulfil your destiny. We won't hurt you now.'

'I'm not Zaister,' he said, for the fourth time. He

68

swallowed. 'You should know. You went by me in the dark, seeking him.'

'Don't be stupid,' she said. 'I sought you alone.'

Kyrast said, 'Of course he is stupid. Men are. Why else should he run away into the magic shadow-place and try to evade us, to no avail. The action of a fool.'

'Where did you find him?' Izvire said.

'About seven miles away. My crow detected him easily. The sorcery had worn out that hid him, or he had worn out. He didn't like *our* magic so well as his own.'

Dekteon went to where the wine ewer stood. He poured out wine for himself into a goblet there and drank.

'Listen,' he said, 'I'll say it once. Zaister was clever in sorcery. He made me look like him, he gave me his clothes. He sent me here by some trick I don't recall properly. This isn't my world.'

'If you have taken Zaister's place,' Kyrast grated, 'where is *he*?'

Dekteon checked. He had not fathomed it before. Now he did. 'I suppose he's become what I was.' He had a sudden awful picture of another man in his body, Zaister as Dekteon, trudging the outlaw woods and hills of earth. He drank again to blot the picture out.

'How dare you,' Izvire whispered in a terrible hiss, 'how dare you presume to drink my wine?'

Dekteon became aware that the cup was silver and the wine white. Moon things. Taboo. He laughed.

'I'm sorry,' he said. 'I told you. I'm not Zaister. I don't know your customs.'

Izvire raised her hand. He perceived she was about to

hit him in the mouth. He caught her wrist; she was strong, but not strong enough. He held her still, and pulled the moon-mask off her face.

She was not like the rest. She was the most beautiful woman he had ever seen. Beautiful, and young. He had expected her to have a harsh aspect, cruel and adamant. Zaister's brain's memory again? Her face was a witch's face all right, sly, intelligent and sharp with rage now. But not evil. Not the face of the thing which had pursued him in the dark.

They stared at each other in gradually dawning amazement.

'Kyrast,' Izvire said, 'he's changed. Is it true? Is he not Zaister?'

'Nonsense,' Kyrast answered, 'he's got clever in his sorcerous shadow-world, wherever he ran to. He's had a year to plot and plan before our powers forced him to come home like a sick dog. It's a grand performance, Sun's Son, I'll give you that. But there have been tricks tried before, in the Last Month, when the consorts feel the cold breath of Night upon them.'

'I didn't know,' Izvire said. She drew her wrist from Dekteon's grasp. She held out her hand for the mask he had snatched. He gave it to her ceremoniously.

'No, you wouldn't,' Kyrast said. 'Your first consort. You'll learn and be more careful with the next. *He* won't escape, I daresay.'

'And who is the next consort, my successor, to be?' Dekteon asked. He spoke negligently. It reminded him of Zaister's way of talking. Perhaps he was going to speak more and more in Zaister's way.

Zaister had been Izvire's first husband. So far, she was innocent of murder.

'Zaister,' Izvire said, 'you must not question me about this. Forget the future.' She turned abruptly from him. To Kyrast she said, 'Did you come on the Pallid, too?'

'No, your husband was alone when we found him. Probably he destroyed it. Some experiment or oversight. Zaister was always wasteful.'

A 'Pallid'? Dekteon thought. What was that?

Izvire clapped her hands.

Through a door, preposterously, came Zaister's servant, White-Face. Yet surely it was not White-Face, could not be?

'Pallid,' Izvire said. Dekteon saw it was the hairless man she had addressed. 'Take Lord Zaister to the Mosaic Room. Then he may return to the Sun's House.'

'Pallid,' Dekteon said, 'an apt name. Do all your Pallids look alike? So – er – *pallid*?'

'You know they do. And what *did* you do with your own Pallid?'

'I didn't,' he said. 'Zaister has it.'

Izvire smiled icily. 'I shan't answer any more. Do as you please until sundown. You weary me.'

She walked across the hall, the crone beside her. A heap of pelts by the ivory chair wriggled and solidified into three snow-white lionesses, which followed the two witches out.

Dekteon drank off the last of the wine. Jauntily he turned to the suitably-titled Pallid, obviously a member of some ugly bald pale race especial to this world.

'Well, then, the Mosaic Room, my friend.'

Definitely, he was talking like Zaister now.

The Mosaic Room had frescoes of flowers and beasts on the walls, mosaics of flowers and beasts on the floor. The ceiling was painted like a sky, one half sunny day, one half moonlit night.

In the middle of the floor, on a pile of cushions and rugs, two black and white women sat playing with a miniscule child. It was about two years of age, a girl; already it had long black hair. Dekteon felt depressed.

He glared at the Pallid reproachfully, somewhat drunkenly.

'Why bring me here?'

'The lord's child. After a year, you wish to see her.'

Dekteon was shocked; shocked as if it really were his own daughter. Bad enough to be saddled with royal rank, a wife, another man's shape, another man's death. A baby as well was just too much.

Yet, despite himself, he was fascinated. The child had no look of Zaister. Already, she was wholly one of the enemy.

He went up, and watched her. She took no notice of him. The two nurses shook rattles at her. In a corner stood a toy lion on rockers – a rocking-lion.

'What's her name?' Dekteon said to the women.

They exchanged a glance. One said, 'The lord forgets the name of his daughter?'

'Yes, the lord forgets.'

The woman pursed her mouth. Dekteon resisted the urge to shake her, then stopped resisting, and shook her hard. The woman squeaked and tumbled sideways. Dekteon seized the uninterested child. Holding her firmly beneath the arms, he whirled her round. He had seen a woodcutter do this with his three-year-old son. It seemed worth trying.

The child, Zaister's child, did not respond. Dekteon whirled her round again. She looked bored. Dekteon set her down, turned about and walked towards the door.

Halfway there, the child called to him, a wordless demand.

He turned.

'Round again,' she said clearly.

'What's your name?' Dekteon said belligerently to the tiny child.

'Vesain,' she snapped, haughty as a woman of twenty.

But when he lifted her up and whirled her once more, she threw back her head and squealed with delight. And when he left, about five minutes later, she began to cry. He felt remorseful. But she was not his.

The priestess Kyrast had gone to her temple, and Izvire was alone but for two lionesses. She paced up and down the long chamber, up and down. And to keep her company the two lionesses paced with her, up and down, up and down. Then they lost the thread, and began a mock-ferocious game in the middle of the floor.

Izvire watched them. She warmed her hands at a brazier.

She was unhappy. As unhappy as a woman can be who is young and quick and has been trained to a life

73

that has no surprises. Everything was mapped out for her. She had no say in it. She was king, yet the religion of her people ruled her. She had no choice.

She had never properly understood her discontent. The life of the Royal Woman, the Moon's Daughter, had always been thus.

Yet Zaister, her first husband, by breaking with tradition and running away, had jolted her into a sense of her own frustration. And now all this absurd talk, this game of his that he was not Zaister but another . . . She almost hated him, though she had loved him in the beginning. And he had responded the way all men of her world, who were loved, responded: like a pleased sleek pet. His life, also, had been decided for him, with no choice. Born with red-gold sun hair, he was trained from his earliest years to become Sun's Son. He took the honour as his right. Only at the end of the fourth year had he seemed to become uneasy. That was usual, of course. Kyrast had given her certain drugs to mix with his food and drink, to ease his trepidation. They had worked, but one day Zaister had caught sight of Izvire mixing a potion in his wine. She had been careless. She did not know why she had been so careless. After that he dined alone. Presently, he withdrew to his palace, to the tower where he amused himself with sorcery, as had countless consorts. It seemed harmless. Then he vanished. For almost a year.

It had been a year of 'disasters'. Rumours spread that the Sun's Son had fled. The people became afraid. Every natural disorder – a storm, a rainless month – was taken as a bad omen. Izvire and the priestesses in turn activated

74

their own sorcery. Zaister had run among shadows, but they traced him. They sent him warnings, and demands. And now, frightened and unable to resist, he had come home to his ordained fate. Yet somehow he really was changed. Not as Izvire remembered.

In her own way, Izvire was afraid of his death. Though it was unavoidably necessary, and though she had no say in it, she pitied him. The fifth day after his sacrifice, the new husband would be brought to her. Already he had been selected, as was traditional, when he was a red-haired handsome child. He had been trained, as Zaister had been trained, to anticipate his role. Izvire had never set eyes on him.

It alarmed her, this wedding to a stranger, not simply once, but once every five years . . . There was another thing. Zaister had been her own age, but the new consort would be five years younger than she. After the next five years, and the next ritual death, the new consort would be ten years younger. Then fifteen. Then twenty. Then—

The Sun's Son could not be permitted to grow old. He would always come to the wedding sixteen years of age.

Now Izvire was young and beautiful and healthy. But, as with Kyrast, who had been Moon's Daughter before her, the years would exact their payment. One morning, Izvire would be going to her marriage with a consort of sixteen, and she would be fifty-one years old.

Zaister had not flinched at the sight of her, nor would the new youth, nor maybe his successor. But she would age, grow thin and bony, begin to lose her sight, perhaps, as Kyrast had. Her escape would come in time. Once

Izvire could no longer bear children, her term as king was over. Then what? She would be elected High Priestess of the Moon, just like Kyrast.

Just like poor withered dry embittered wicked old Kyrast.

The women of this world were not given to tears. Izvire, instead, whistled her lionesses to heel, and called a Pallid to saddle her lion.

Only Royal Women and priestesses might ride the male red lion, the Sun animal. Even the consort was not permitted to ride him. Possibly that was why she wanted to go riding suddenly, to remind herself of who she was.

She wondered if Zaister had visited the child, their daughter.

She wondered, and wondered.

Dekteon wondered, as he rode his bear-horse up the Royal Road, behind the Pallid, about why he still did not feel afraid.

Obviously, the body he was in was not merely a replica of Zaister's body. It *was* Zaister's body. Dekteon had got used to Zaister's sorcery. He no longer puzzled over it. So, the body felt at home here in this world. Only the threat of death upset it. Strangely, that was what Dekteon found easiest to ignore.

He was not going to die, it was that simple.

He had avoided death in the copper mines, which had been pretty certain. He could avoid this death.

The Royal Road was a private route stretching from the Moon Palace to the Sun's House. The Pallid, who exactly resembled White-Face, trotted ahead to lead the way.

If Dekteon relaxed his own mind, stopped thinking his own thoughts, perhaps Zaister's brain's memory would become stronger, revealing all manner of useful knowledge.

It seemed to Dekteon he had got more clever since he had been in Zaister's body. More witty and elegant in the way he spoke.

Across the path bounded a red lion, a woman mounted on it, two white lionesses pacing behind.

Izvire, her hair streaming, a bow and quiver slung from her shoulders, rode off among the flower trees without a glance at him.

SEVEN

Sun's House

As with his journey here, and the situation of the city itself, the Sun's House was familiar. Like the ruined mansion, it was located on the summit of a hill. The Royal Road led up the hill to it as the paved track had led to the ruin. There was a wall with towers, not four but ten. The towers had windows of multi-coloured glass, and gold discs were set on the wedge-shaped tower-tops. The whole of the courtyard was a garden, not merely on the north-west and south-west sides of the house. But leading from the gate was the same avenue of marble statues – lions and dogs. This time they were intact, the serpentine lions had horns, and the winged dogs were also equipped with six legs. Dekteon started to laugh.

Ignoring the Pallid, who was trotting towards the main door, Dekteon urged his bear-horse through the trees into the area where the garden of the mansion had been. Sure enough, he soon discovered a pool and a fountain. The awful face of the fountain was really a macabre representation of the sun, surrounded by rays.

The Moon Garden had been white. This Sun Garden was crimson and saffron. The trees were of a new spreading kind, many double-trunked.

In a paved space, Dekteon came on a small, open-sided building of pillars supporting a tiled roof – the approximation of the garden shrine. However, there were no bakehouses or smithies to be seen. There was a stable, though. The Pallid, when Dekteon found him, took the bear-horse to this stable and gave it to other Pallids, just like himself.

Indeed, the house into which Dekteon now walked swarmed with Pallids, all identical to each other and to his guide. The women must keep an exact note of their number, however, for they had registered that Zaister's Pallid was missing.

'How do I tell you apart?' Dekteon asked the guide.

'There will be no requirement, lord, to tell us apart. Summon us and we will come.'

'But which of you will come?'

'It does not matter, lord.'

'Yes, it does,' said Dekteon. He instinctively sympathised for a moment with these slaves. To be called 'Red' and whipped for your insolence was better than total lack of individuality. 'I shan't beat you,' said Dekteon, reluctantly enjoying his novel position as a master. 'Tell me your name.'

'I have no name.'

It struck Dekteon how mechanical and precise the speech and actions of all the Pallids were. White-Face had unnerved him in the ruin. And White-Face . . . there was something about White-Face that had scared

Dekteon. At one point, hadn't he made himself look like someone else? Dekteon couldn't recall. He shrugged it off, and said to the static Pallid, 'I'm going to call you "Fren". If I call for you by name, I want *you* to come, and no other, Fren. Do you understand?'

'Yes,' said the Pallid, 'Fren.'

It was a childish joke, but Dekteon was amused. ('Here, Fren, do up my boot-buckles. There, Fren, saddle my horse.')

Dekteon went through the Sun's House alone. Definitely it was the original of Zaister's ruin, though larger. There were more rooms, other floors. And it was attractive and airy, which the ruin had not been; or perhaps it had, to start with, before the women's magic eroded Zaister's. At length Dekteon identified the secret tower, or its equivalent. The door was of bronze and, in this world, not locked.

He went in, up the stairs, and came to a doorway sealed by another bronze door. There was a handle but it did not turn. In the door itself was the shape of a man's right hand; Zaister's hand. Which meant, surely, that there was a spell on the door so it would open only at the touch of Zaister's hand inside the print. Dekteon recollected that his hand now *was* Zaister's hand.

He pressed his palm into the print. There was a sighing noise, and the door flew open.

The chamber was round with a high ceiling. A window still faced south-east, as in the ruin. But in the ruin the chamber had been bare. Now – now it was the laboratory of a sorcerer, and no mistaking it. Probably it had even been like this in the ruin, and Zaister had hidden it from Dekteon, somehow.

The walls were painted in a thousand symbols, numerals and pictures. To Dekteon they meant everything, and nothing. He could not read. They could have been the diagrams of his own world marked there, and he would not have known them. But there were other things. Tall chests of bronze, each closed, with a hand-print in the metal doors. Exactly before the window stood an amber crystal mounted on a stand. Shadows and mists seemed to come and go over its surface. They might have been reflections of the light. Curving round the northern portion of the room was a metal bench, with implements and objects strewn around. A movement caught Dekteon's startled eye: the perfectly-articulated model of a golden bird was picking about there, strutting and poking with its beak. Without warning, it flew up into the air with a clap of metal wings. It flashed past Dekteon's face, and up on to the top of one of the higher chests, out of his reach. It seemed to regard him from gemmed eye-sockets. Unnerved, Dekteon stepped back, and collided with a bronze lever that protruded from one side of the bench.

At once a shutter opened in the ceiling. A silken rope came falling straight down out of it, till it brushed the floor. The source of the rope and the rope's upper part remained hidden in the gloom above.

Dekteon, intimidated but curious, seized the rope's inviting end and prepared to climb. Instantly the rope jerked back into motion. Alarmed, he almost let go of it, but clung on wildly. The rope drew him up, through the ceiling-shutter, into an empty vault above. Empty, that is, save for one thing.

A chariot and team stood in the upper room. The horses were of the bear-foot, horned type, the chariot had three great wheels. The whole thing was made of shining gold.

The ridiculous gold bird flew up through the shutter. It whizzed round Dekteon's head. Involuntarily he struck out at it. The bird dodged expertly and landed on the chariot rail.

'Kyrast is a hag,' said the gold bird. 'Izvire is a fool. Zaister is clever, Zaister is handsome. Zaister is king.'

It must be some toy of Zaister's. Yes, Dekteon could imagine Zaister listening to this hollow praise in the safety of his locked room.

The bird perched on a wheel of the chariot. Another toy?

Dekteon mounted the chariot. He put his hands on the inflexible reins. The bird squawked and clapped away.

There was a jolt. The chariot began to move, although there was nowhere it could move to, here in the vaulted roof of the tower.

The golden bear-horses galloped. The wheels sizzled. Dekteon felt the speed, felt a wind rush past his face. The walls spun. Amazed, exhilarated, Dekteon braced himself against the tautened reins, the bouncing floor of the vehicle. It was the link he needed.

Suddenly, Dekteon became Zaister. At least, he *knew* Zaister, from the *inside*. Every memory and every art of Zaister's had left its signature in Zaister's brain.

And now Dekteon gained astounding access to it, just as he had vaguely dreamed he might.

Holding to the golden reins of the racing, motionless chariot, Dekteon, the ignorant and uneducated slave, became a sorcerer. As easily and as crazily as that.

Zaister had been six years old when the priestesses came. They wore black and silver and rode on lions, and a few male warriors rode with them. The leader of the priestesses, the predecessor of Kyrast, was still a hag. It was well known the Royal Women who became the High Priestesses of the Moon did not age well. But Zaister did not know this, only that the women frightened him.

He cried, and his father comforted him. But his mother told him sternly to be quiet.

His mother and the High Priestess talked a while in the Great Room of the house. Then Zaister was summoned.

He was examined. He sobbed softly all the time. At last, the High Priestess called him to her. She gave him a sugar-apple, and patted him brusquely on the head. Zaister stopped crying and blossomed under her attention. The Priestess said something to Zaister's mother and she fell to her knees; Zaister was surprised to see his fearless mother overcome. Then the High Priestess went to the window and shouted the same thing out into the street. A lot of people must have gathered there, for a huge roar went up. It was the first time Zaister heard that roar. He did not understand it then.

Zaister's father came to him and led him away, and his father was crying now, trying to hide it from the boy. It was all a mystery.

Soon, however, Zaister discovered that he was special. He was not expected to learn his father's trade – his father was a sculptor – nor to attend school with the other sons of the city. Instead, private tutors came to the house. Also, whenever he went out, people would bow to him in the streets. Sometimes they would bring him gifts – a toy horse, a box of sweets. Even women of consequence would sometimes notice him. 'Is this the new First Consort of the little king?'

Zaister started to realize, slowly, and then very fast, that he was the second most important male in the city, the most important, naturally, being the current Sun's Son, the husband of the current king. But Zaister was to be Sun Consort himself, and an especially vital one. For he would be the first husband of the next king, Izvire. The first husband of a king was always reared more carefully than his successors, since a new king meant a new era, a New Moon and a New Sun beginning together.

As for the ritual sacrifice, Zaister did not actually grasp that part of it. He was aware consorts vanished after five years and had to be replaced, but the event was always spoken of as one of glory and blessing. An extra treat at the end of a consort's term.

When Zaister was eleven, the priestesses, who had occasionally visited him so that he was now accustomed to them, conducted him to the Sun's House. How proud Zaister was, riding through the streets and avenues. The crowds flocked to see him and sent up their passionate roar of approval.

In the magnificence of the Sun's House, Zaister was taught fresh lessons. His duties and responsibilities to the king and to the religion, and to the people. He began to wear fine clothes, and preened himself happily in them. He was given horses to ride. He was tutored in sorcery. It was as much a tradition that the consort be a sorcerer as that the king be a sorceress. The consort was supposed to amuse himself with sorcery while the king carried on her weighty affairs of state. It was another toy. Yet Zaister showed exceptional aptitude. His basic intelligence, stifled by the cosseted life the city forced on him, fastened on sorcery with eagerness.

It was a cunning habit with all consorts, somehow to keep them from the notion of death, as it really was. A consort never saw death, animal or human. He was not allowed to hunt, being too precious to be risked. No funeral might pass below his windows. Death was never spoken of in his presence.

One day, Zaister was loitering in a grove beside the Royal Road. He should not have been there, but a gossiping male tutor had let slip that Izvire often took the Royal Road when returning from riding in the forests beyond the city. Zaister was curious and nervous. He hid in the grove several days, hoping to catch sight of Izvire, but with no success. And this day, it seemed, would be the same.

It drew on to a peaceful noon, warm and pleasant. Zaister had no premonition under the scented trees by the road. Suddenly a girl of his own age, fifteen, came riding along. She had companions with her, all young girls like herself, but something told him she was Izvire, his future wife. Zaister stared through the leaves. So he saw what hung from a pole between two of the mounted lions. It was the carcase of a stag, a red stag with branching male antlers. It was not messy, for the pack of lionesses killed quickly and cleanly, but it was unmistakably dead.

And in that moment, fifteen years of age, Zaister knew that he, too, was going to die, and maybe not so cleanly, the prey of Izvire and the women. And sick terror closed on his heart.

Just for a month then, before his pleasure-loving nature over-laid it, terror stayed with him. Eventually, he seemed able to forget, because he had to.

Several years he kept fear at bay, kept it at bay until fear was very close. Until the fourth year of his five year term.

The women were cruel and powerful. Their religion was the same. He did not want to die. If it had been in battle . . . He had never fought a battle, that would probably have scared him just as much, if the truth were admitted — but a sacrifice: no! Zaister, ignoring the fate of all the red-haired men who had died before him, determined to escape.

And escape he did.

Dekteon left the chariot. He knew how to halt it now, by pressure on a concealed knob. Bemused, he let himself down by the rope into the room below. The noisy bird he captured and quietened by snapping shut its beak and wings. Then he sat on the window-sill and gazed through the coloured glass, unseeing, at the city.

He understood Zaister, could not help it. He understood the city, its geography and its attitudes, or as much as Zaister had understood. Oddly, Dekteon really had become Zaister, yet still he was Dekteon. Suddenly he had access to Zaister's memory and emotions, was able to use all Zaister's store of intelligence and magic – but none of Zaister's weakness had touched Dekteon's mind. Perhaps, if it were true what the priests of Dekteon's world said, that men had souls, then the *body* was Zaister's, but the *soul* was Dekteon's, and that was what made the difference.

Dekteon gave up puzzling.

With a very vocal yell of triumph, he strode out of the magic room – grown preposterously familiar to him; no need to look in chests, he knew what was in them – and down the stairs of the tower.

He noticed, having reached the Great Room below, that the sun was westering. Since he had learned, from Zaister's memory, the length of the day, he was aware he had lost track of time rather than the day being short. In fact, days and nights in this world were a few hours longer than in his own.

A Pallid stood in the room. It might be the one he had named Fren or it might not. It didn't matter. As he was now informed, the Pallids themselves were the products of sorcery. They were not human, as were the servants he had seen about the city. Exclusive to the Moon Palace and the Sun's House, the Pallids were slaves in the sense that they carried out any tasks given them with precision. But that was all. They were strange dolls, set going by clockwork. Like Zaister's golden bird.

'Well, Fren, my friend,' said Dekteon casually to the Pallid, slipping naturally into the speech mode of Zaister, not without amusement. 'High time I prepared myself for dinner.'

They walked through a colonnade, well remembered by Zaister's brain, in the reddening light. After bathing in a tub of crystal with gold taps, he found clothing laid out for him, of splendid russet velvet.

Dekteon smiled. Not hurrying, though the sun was on the brink of the horizon, he went back up into the tower. He set out certain instruments, and drew certain symbols on a sheet of parchment. Then he stripped off the clothes and hung them ready.

As he worked the spell, his eyes went over the walls. He could read every diagram written there. He could write. Before, he had not even been able to write his own name, just the first letter.

The spell was quite a simple one. Zaister had played with it once, to alter a green bird to a white one. It had to do with light and the spectrum. A shift around in the particles of the material of Dekteon's clothes was all that was required. Dekteon smiled again. Zaister would never have dared.

Presently, as the sun sank, Dekteon came down from the tower once more, the golden bird under his arm.

The Pallid, or another Pallid, opened the doors for him. Dekteon strolled out from the Sun's House, on to the Royal Road.

With a combination of Zaister's pride and Dekteon's

rebellion, the young man pondered, with grim pleasure, on how he would be received.

For the Sun's Son had changed his clothes to the wrong colour, for dinner. He was clad in the taboo black, exclusive to the Daughters of Night.

EIGHT

Sorcery by Night and Day

The Moon Palace was bright with round white alabaster lamps. Each lamp was a reminder of the moon itself. Dinner was to be served in the Great Room of the palace, and tables had been set there. Certain women of importance and their husbands, and members of Izvire's household were present, also three priestesses led by Kyrast. When Dekteon entered, unescorted and in black, absolute silence fell.

It was Kyrast who spoke first. Across the length of the room she cawed, in her harsh crow's voice:

'Don't you know, Sun's Son, you're unlawfully dressed?'

'Am I?' asked Dekteon. 'How?'

Kyrast just pointed at him. Zaister's memory told him her sight was considerably better than he had once thought. She could see shapes and colours quite clearly.

'I don't understand,' said Dekteon.

Kyrast snapped her fingers impatiently.

'You understand, Zaister. And you act like a baby. All men are the same.' She tilted her head away in obvious

90

disgust. 'If it's your silly baby's whim to blaspheme, you must do it. It'll make no difference in the end, I assure you.'

The other people took their lead from the High Priestess. They attempted to ignore Dekteon's black. Plainly, however, they were ill at ease.

At that moment, a curtain was pulled aside and Izvire entered. She was attended by a group of girl companions. Three or four lionesses, as usual, loped at her heels.

When Izvire took in Dekteon, she froze.

She was not wearing her moon-mask, it hung from her girdle. He saw her face go the grey-white of flour. Then she screamed at him.

'How *dared* you— To come into my sight as you are!' She gathered herself, and cried, 'I'll have you taken out and whipped, you mannerless clot!'

Dekteon knew that the sacred consort could not be whipped. It was not permitted. For the first time in his life he could ignore the threat of a lashing.

Coolly he said, 'You forget yourself, my lady.'

'I am not your lady, I am your king!' she shouted.

Dekteon decided to unremember she was there. Instead, he took the gold bird from under his arm, opened its beak and wings and tossed it in the air. It whirled into mad flight. The dinner guests ducked in some confusion.

Now Izvire's face was flushed. She strode across to him. She said, 'You will beg my pardon and the pardon of the priestess Kyrast. Then you will go and change your garments.'

Dekteon looked in her eyes, a fraction lower than his own.

'Surely it's time we ate?' he said.

He thought she might lose control still further, but she didn't. Suddenly, she was a model of calm, though the little smile she gave him was like a little razor. She glanced about at the guests. 'I apologise for my husband. It's his fancy. But we'll indulge him, won't we?'

The guests rustled nervously.

'Nice to have someone to apologise for you,' Dekteon remarked. 'One could do almost anything . . .'

The gold bird flashed over again. He reached up and caught it.

Izvire went to the upper table and sat down. Kyrast was seated at her right hand. Zaister-Dekteon's place would be on the left.

Dekteon joined them and sat too. The guests sat. Pallids were already coming up with dishes. Even in this, taboos were observed. White meat for the women, red for the men. Dekteon put the bird on the table and pressed the raised feather he had accidently pressed before. The bird bowed and declaimed: 'Kyrast is a hag. Izvire is a fool. Zaister is clever, Zaister is handsome. Zaister is king.'

A second ghastly hush descended. Some of the women at the table paled. Some broke the taboo, and reddened.

Izvire said in a tight voice, 'The child must play with his toys.'

Kyrast broke a piece of bread with the sound of a whiplash.

One of Izvire's companions – a sort of girl-guard, hissed, 'Let us take him outside, my king.'

Dekteon beamed at the girl. 'Why not?'

Izvire said loudly, 'The eastern harvest will be a good one this year, and the northern better. But there are getting to be too many wolves in the forests. We shall have to have a hunt.'

'I,' said Dekteon, 'killed a wolf once. Not like your wolves. No horns. Still, a wolf. It was when I was seventeen. A great hunt at By-the-Lake.'

'A wolf?' Izvire laughed. All the women, except Kyrast, laughed. 'My Zaister never slew anything in his whole life.'

'You're forgetting. I'm not Zaister.'

'Yes. So I am.'

Something cold and sharp slid against Dekteon's neck. One of the companion girls had come behind his chair and laid a knife beside his windpipe. 'Can I get you something, lord,' she said, 'to ease your cough?'

Zaister had never disarmed anyone, let alone a woman. Dekteon, veteran if not always victor of many a brawl with fellow slaves, lurched forward, then spun round, knocking his chair over and bringing up an arm to send the girl's blade flying. She had not reckoned on retaliation. He caught her by the wrist, swung her up, and bore her, kicking and threatening, to the doors. He threw her outside quite gently. Then slammed the doors shut in her face.

He assumed she would run in again next minute, but she did not. Bewildered or shamed, she failed to return to the dinner.

Izvire and the guests, with much show, ignored all this.

Dekteon sat down again. They were talking about the planting of fig trees – the figs here were white – along the southern perimeter of the city. Agriculture was a huge concern. Even the city had been made of green silica to represent vegetable growth.

Black and white fruit was being offered to the women. A Pallid offered Dekteon a scarlet citrus. The gold bird patrolled the bread trencher. Nobody touched it.

'Then there is the apple plain,' Izvire said.

'And where is the plain that I am to die on?' Dekteon said clearly.

Izvire's hand clenched upon her table knife. He supposed it was her anger. Then she put her other hand up over her eyes, and leaned her head on it. He saw her hands were both convulsively trembling.

But she mastered herself. Looking up, she said, 'It was a hard hot ride this afternoon. You must forgive me.' She gazed bleakly about at the women. The men had lowered their eyes in alarm. 'I think I shall go to my bed.'

Izvire rose. Another noiseless ripple went over the diners.

Dekteon realized that, as consort, he was meant to go with her.

He felt an acid amusement, more intense and malevolent than the other.

'Don't think, lady,' he said, 'you'll find me lying beside you tonight.'

No one said a word.

Izvire turned and walked out, her beasts and girls going after.

Dekteon felt momentarily sorry for her. But Zaister's memories of Izvire, all adoring fright, filled Dekteon with angry contempt, for Zaister and for the woman.

He swivelled in his chair and offered the red citrus to a portly female. She immediately got up and stumped out. The rest of the diners were quick to follow.

Soon Dekteon found himself alone at the tables with the crone-priestess Kyrast.

Spitefully he flicked the feather of the golden bird.

'*Kyrast is a hag*!'

'So she is,' Kyrast grated. 'Let's see,' she added, 'three taboos broken so far: wear Night's colour. Insult the king. Insult the priestess. What's left to do, eh?'

'Enough,' he said.

'You're too quick. Do you know what happened to the too-quick fox? He saw something move, and bit off his own tail. When you were twelve years old,' said Kyrast, 'you made a bronze bird just like that gold one.'

'No,' he said. 'I was thirteen. And it couldn't talk. Or fly.'

Kyrast struck the flat of her gristly hand on the table.

'So! Excellent memory. I wanted to be certain. But you're Zaister, and no doubt, despite your denials. Bitten your tail, foxy?'

Dekteon had spoken without thinking, saying 'I'.

'I have access to Zaister's memory,' said Dekteon. 'I've altered since I've been here, in Zaister's body. It's sorcery.'

'No,' she said, 'the hag isn't convinced. You're a fool.

Like the others. I weathered eight husbands when I was king. All idiots.'

A chill ran across Dekteon's shoulders. Eight. Eight dead men.

'Did you regret them?' he said.

'Every one,' she said. 'But the Sun's Son must die. He cannot grow old. Not old like Kyrast.'

'Because disaster would overtake the land if the Sun's Son lived beyond his term?'

'Disaster for sure.'

'The crops would fail?' Dekteon said. 'The sun would go out?'

'And more,' she said. 'If the consort failed to die, the first calamities would occur in a day, or less. Darkening of the sun, hurricane winds, upheavals of the earth. By the fifth day, the day on which the king should marry her new consort when the old is gone, the world would be shattered and empty.' He wondered if she actually believed it. 'And now. Go up to Izvire.'

'Not yet,' he said.

'You haven't long,' she said. 'Make the most of it.'

'I mean to.'

Kyrast got to her feet slowly. Her ancient bones clacked as she straightened. Her part-blind eyes stared at him. There was a shimmer over the lamplight. Kyrast was gone. In her place, for a few seconds, stood a flickering two-dimensional illusion – a beautiful girl, with long black hair. It might almost have been Izvire.

'That's how I used to look,' Kyrast said. 'See the resemblance? Hard to recall otherwise that I'm Izvire's mother. I wonder,' she said, shimmering back in quick horrible stages to her solid crone-shape, letting the illusion slip. 'I wonder if it's worse to die young, and nobly, for the people, Sun's Son. Or to live and wither into this.'

Dekteon walked in the Moon Garden under the moon. He should have avoided the moonlight. He was a man.

He came on another fountain. He recognised it. It was the counterpart of the fountain he had tried to drink at when he fled across Zaister's ruinous valley. It had run wine or run dry. Now only water came from the spout. At the edge of the basin, the liquid was barely disturbed by the fountain. Dekteon looked in and saw himself reflected. Or rather, saw reflected the body and face and hair of Zaister.

In fact, as Zaister had noted, the two men were almost identical in any case. The thing was that Dekteon had never properly seen himself, to make the comparison. Zaister, on the other hand, had often gazed in mirrors. Zaister's brain was able to tell Dekteon now how small the difference was between what he had been and what he had become.

No wonder he had felt drawn to Zaister, felt he would serve him willingly. Zaister was his twin, his other self.

Somewhere, someone screamed.

Dekteon stared around at the Moon Palace. He knew who had screamed. A child. His daughter – no, Zaister's daughter.

He started to pound along the paths back towards the building. The screams went on, but they were lusty: temper rather than fear.

He could locate the Mosaic Room easily from this side of the Palace. He got there quickly, flung back the doors, and was inside.

The scene he interrupted was both comic and appalling. Three bowls stood on the floor amid a litter of combs, spatulas and cloths. The child, with her hair wet, stood at bay in a corner. The two nurses were threatening and cajoling, to no avail.

They had been about to dye her hair. Dye it black, though she was only two years old. She must be fair then. Or red, like Zaister himself. Yes, that was logical, a girl often took her father's colouring. But Zaister had not known. That meant — Dekteon scowled — the hair of the child called Vesain had been dyed since it first grew out.

Vesain had caught sight of Dekteon. She stopped screaming and, like her mother, became suddenly completely calm. She regarded him quizzically, intrigued by him.

'That's better, Vesain,' said one of the nurses. 'Such a tantrum. Come here now, it will soon be done.'

'No,' Dekteon said, 'it will not.' The women glared at him. They saw his black garments at last, and exclaimed. 'Yes, yes,' Dekteon said. He went to the child. He put his hand on her hair. Being wet, it was flattened to the scalp, and he saw the hint of non-black roots. It was like a blow struck for him in this unfriendly world. 'Vesain,' he said, 'I am taking you for a ride. To the Sun's House.'

The child climbed into his arms, and let him carry her away while the nurses clamoured.

He carried her along Royal Road on his shoulder, into the Sun's House, up to the tower room and behind the door. There, almost casually, he worked the colour spell again. The black faded from the child's hair. It was too easy. Why didn't Izvire use her own sorcery, instead of dye, on her daughter? Another taboo, perhaps. He did not trouble to remember.

Vesain's natural hair was the colour of corn sheaves on fire. She seemed pleased with it, but fell asleep making breath-mist in the bronze mirror. He put her in his own bed in the Sun chamber, tucked her in its hugeness. She was a pretty brat, but he wasn't sure what he would do with her. Probably, he thought, it would be best to return her to her nurses in the morning.

Just then, thirty warrior guard hammered on the door below.

A slave opened up, and the guard tramped into the Great Room. They said Izvire summoned Zaister. They were respectful but insistent.

'All right,' Dekteon said.

He and they went all the way back to the Moon Palace, leaving Vesain asleep, with her father's toy gold bird perched on the pillow.

He sat in an ante-room. Izvire kept him waiting an hour at least. He was bored, but not intimidated as Zaister would have been. Dekteon knew quite well what she was at.

At last, she came out. She was wearing a black robe and her moon-mask to impress him.

Dekteon grinned.

'What have you done with my daughter?' she demanded.

'Our daughter.' He realized what he had said, but did not bother to correct it. 'She's in the Sun's House.'

'You have no business and no right to take her there.'

'Well,' he said, 'never mind.'

He sensed the tension in Izvire. She positively sizzled with it.

'Listen,' she said, 'you've done enough to anger me already. Don't do anything else.'

'Why, what will you do? Nothing, of course. Not till next Full Moon.'

'Why did you take the child?'

'To alter the colour of her hair to what it should be.'

'*Alter* the colour?'

'Yes.'

'How?'

'The same way I changed my clothing to black.' As he said it, he realized, with a slight shock, that the women had not actually mastered this spell. Could it be that, in certain magics, Zaister had been more clever even than the women? Before he could pursue the notion, she began speaking again.

'Why must you do these things? They help no one. They don't help you.' She sounded as though she were almost pleading with him.

'My – Zaister's daughter,' he said, 'doesn't like being dyed. And not surprising.' An abrupt thought struck him. 'What happens to a black-haired *man* in this city? More dye?' Another thought, colder than the first: 'What happens if the king bears a son rather than a daughter?'

'I have never borne a son,' Izvire rasped at him.

'But if you had, what? Do you expose him, perhaps, like the poor woman who can't afford to feed another mouth? Or just smother him in his cot.'

'You're disgusting!' she shouted. 'You know a king's son becomes a Sun priest, or a warrior – whichever he wishes. You *know* this.' It was true, he did know, now. 'You know, yet you say these lies to infuriate me.' Her voice broke. Suddenly she said, 'Do you think I love my life? I don't. I hate it. But you and I, we have our roles. We can't escape. Oh, Zaister,' she said, much softer, 'let me get drugs from Kyrast, the drugs that make the consort forget what is to come.'

'Go to die smiling,' he said.

'Don't you believe what we are taught, that the dead consort journeys to the lands of the sun? To perpetual pleasure and happiness.'

'No,' he said. 'Do you?'

'Zaister,' she said. It occurred to him that a woman in his own world would have been crying by now. This one could not cry. But the tears were there, just the same.

He went to her, and put an arm round her.

'What I believe is this. Zaister was a brilliant sorcerer, who could have outwitted you, and the priestess, and all the Daughters of Night. He even did it, up to a point. What held him back was his fear of you all, instilled in him from his childhood. He was convinced he couldn't fight you, so he ran, instead. If he *had* fought you, on your own ground, with weapons like your own, I think he'd have won. What then, Izvire?'

'*You* are Zaister,' she said flatly. She ignored his arm, but did not move away.

'Well then,' Dekteon said, 'if I'm Zaister, and I'm so clever, you'd better watch out.'

He was happy in the morning. He thought she seemed happy, too. He had stayed with her for the last of the night. It had happened without fuss or unease, despite the drama before.

As at the beginning, each was ambushed by surprise at the qualities of the other.

In the pink sun rays that fell over the bed, they looked at each other solemnly. She did not kiss him like his king, but like his wife.

Later, they went riding. Not on lions or horses, but in a chariot drawn by white tigers, such as Dekteon had seen on his arrival.

The fields beyond the northern wall of the city gave way to great forests. The trees were a hundred shades of colour. In a clearing, a waterfall hung like a glistening rod between sky and earth. ·

They did not talk much. At least, they did not talk about important things, such as religion, death or anger.

They ate bread and fruit near the waterfall. He saw her touch at a pendant on one of her bracelets – he had got used to their sound by now. He guessed the pendant was hollow, and contained some drug she already had from Kyrast, to 'make the consort forget what was to come'. But she didn't attempt to use it.

There were two flasks of wine; one white, which was hers, one gold – his.

She looked at them dubiously, then at him. He gave the flask of gold wine to her.

'Who's to see?'

She laughed unexpectedly. She drank the wine of the Sun's Son. When he drank her white wine, she laughed again.

He supposed it was one step in the right direction.

Part Three

NINE

The Hunt

Zaister woke with an awareness of awful dread. But it could only have been a dream of the past, for the moment he opened his eyes and became conscious of his surroundings, the dread faded swiftly.

Zaister – it was the real Zaister – stretched luxuriously. He was used to stretching this way, after a night in a soft bed. Now, however, the stretch was stiff and painful. He had been lying in a damp narrow cave on a hillside. The fire was long out. A rock had ground into his back. He was hungry, and his mouth was parched.

Fortunately, Dekteon's body, the body Zaister now occupied, was used to such hardships.

Zaister took the bronze mirror from the chest and examined himself – or Dekteon's self. Hard tanned flesh and dark clay-red hair. One of the bottom teeth was chipped from a blow in the mouth . . . Still, not a bad appearance. Very like Zaister as he had been. At least, a healthy body that would not be sacrificed in a month's time.

Zaister laughed aloud. He worked his shoulders,

winced at the feel of Dekteon's latest beating. His face was also scratched. He shouted for the Pallid.

The Pallid came, bringing water from a nearby stream in the gold cup; the wine had soured during its transference from the between-world place to this. The water was cold and iron-tasting. Zaister sipped it without pleasure, while the Pallid rubbed salve into the healing stripes on his back.

It was bizarre. Dekteon's brain remembered getting that beating, and so Zaister was able to 'remember' it too. Actually, Zaister had not realized this would happen. He had thought that his mind would dominate the brain of Dekteon, and all Dekteon's remembrances and characteristics would automatically be wiped out. This was not the case. It was odd. Like being two men at once.

Really, Zaister understood very little altogether about this miracle he had achieved. Like many a cunning sorcerer, he had stumbled on a fabulous new magic. The between-place, the bridge between parallel worlds, he had found first. He had been experimenting with the amber Vision Crystal when he had glimpsed in it an area of mist, and in the mist strange shapes, that seemed to take on whatever form he thought of – trees, buildings, beasts. That had been in the fourth year. It began only as a genius-game, but ended as a desperate bid for survival. He had investigated the ancient libraries of the city. He had read the theories of sage-sorcerers, and learned of the idea of a Vortex Gate, by which a man might enter a parallel world. And find his own 'twin' – himself in another life. Zaister constructed a

Vortex Gate, its central chamber and its circle of power-conducting stones. He reached the world of mist, the between-place. And beyond that, in truth, saw a parallel world – which he could not reach as he was. Then he had searched, half-disbelieving still, till he found Dekteon. When Zaister actually found Dekteon, his 'twin', Zaister had known that he could escape.

Zaister yawned. He wondered how Dekteon was making out in that world ruled by the Daughters of Night. Not well, probably. Poor Dekteon. Zaister felt sentimental sorrow for the human being he had manoeuvred, duped and sent to his death. Then the sorrow passed off.

The Pallid had stopped applying the salve. It was moving sluggishly. It had been in this world before, posing as the old slave at By-the-Lake. Perhaps this world did not suit it, was gradually ruining it, as it had ruined the food and wine Zaister had tried to bring with him. Zaister stood up, and set his hands on the Pallid and spoke an incantation over it. A grinding noise came from inside it, as it responded. Maybe Zaister would have to remove the white metal plate in its belly and readjust the Pallid's mechanism. That would be a nuisance. He didn't have the proper tools any more, would have to instruct some person in this world on how to make them for him.

Zaister laced up his shirt and tunic. He wore the same embroidered red and bronze gear he had given Dekteon to wear out of his own wardrobe. The garments were getting muddy. In the chest, which the Pallid would carry, were ten other magnificent suits, cloaks, boots and jewellery, gold plate and similar items. Better save the finery. The Sun knew how long he would have to tramp about in this drab wilderness.

Zaister went outside the cave. Yes, it was surely a dull world, this. Everything looked grey and dun to him, even the reds and greens were dim. And the sun was pale, nearly white in the autumn sky.

Zaister did not feel at home here. He felt uneasy.

Still, he would find shelter soon. Barter some jewel, or simply set his powerful personality to work to achieve what he wanted. Everything would be all right. You could get used to most things.

On top of the hill he could see the remains of the Vortex Gate he had made pass through from the between-place: a circle of bleak leaning stones, at the centre a broken slab of granite, and a mound of upturned earth. Like a disturbed grave.

Zaister said something to the stones. It took them slightly longer to disappear than he would have expected. Another effect of this monochrome world?

Zaister walked off across the monochrome world. The Pallid came after, bowed, blank-faced, beneath the weight of the chest.

Half an hour later, Zaister and the Pallid had crossed the river. It was the river Zaister had instructed the Pallid to tell Dekteon about, when in the guise of the old slave at By-the-Lake. In fact, it was some miles farther on than the 'old slave' had suggested. A rickety bridge spanned the water. On the other side was rough heath-land, patched with copses of trees.

Zaister was already tired of the walk, but Dekteon's strong body strode easily. An icy wind blew at Zaister's back. He made the Pallid stop, and opened the chest. He took out the cloak of red wool lined with wolf-skin, and put it on.

If this land really were outlaw country, Zaister had no notion. The story that it was had been a fabrication, to make Dekteon want to escape in this direction. The night before, Zaister had seen a glow of distant light that seemed to indicate a town or city. He was making for that.

Noon came and went. Zaister was impatiently hungry. He plucked some berries, but spat them out in revulsion. Perhaps all the fruit was vile in this world. At length, he sat down in the half-hearted shelter of a tree, and sent the Pallid hunting. Pallids were excellent for this, able to move very stealthily when told to. Also, being non flesh, they had no smell to alert wild beasts.

The Pallid crept off. A few minutes later Zaister picked out the hollow noise of baying hounds on the wind.

Zaister jumped to his feet. He knew instantly. Dekteon's brain remembered the cry of Lord Fren's dogs as they hunted him. This cry was the same.

Zaister had reckoned on the hunt having been abandoned. The hounds had followed Dekteon into the ring of stones. They had pawed and howled about the granite block, digging up the soil. The men had hacked up the block itself and found the hole beneath empty. Dekteon was beyond them all by then.

No master was going to pursue a quarry who

vanished into thin air, leaving no scent. What could have happened? Zaister tried to reason it out. Maybe Fren and his party had camped near by. A dog had slipped its leash, gone wandering, found a *new* trail of man scent.

Zaister was afraid. Outwardly he was Dekteon. Neither dog nor man would see the difference. For a second Zaister panicked. The answer to this trouble was sorcery, but he had nothing easily to hand. The tower room, and its equivalent in the between-place, were gone. Certain instruments were packed in the chest. But he needed parchment, fires, more than anything – time.

Suddenly, all the quick spells stored in his mind seemed to dissolve. The cry of the hounds came more loudly. Zaister stared back the way he had come. He could glimpse nothing yet. But they were this side of the river, that was for sure.

Zaister shouted for the Pallid. Then again. Presently it appeared. It had caught a rabbit but not killed it. The Pallid held it out to Zaister, a heap of quivering mushroom-brown fur.

'Leave that!' Zaister cried. 'Pick up the chest and run. This way.'

The Pallid let go of the rabbit, which crouched motionless with terror in the grass. Zaister thought of the black rabbits, sinister sentinels of the priestesses, which had escorted Dekteon in his flight. Then he, too, turned to fly.

The Pallid obediently ran with him. Bowed beneath the chest, it staggered drunkenly.

There must be some magic, some small stupid magic, that he could devise to throw the dogs off his scent.

Nothing would come. If he had had the amber Vision Crystal with him, through which he had been able to work illusions – but the original Crystal was in the tower of the Sun's House, and its more feeble duplicate in the tower of the between-place; both large immovable fixtures. He had planned to create another, had not thought it would be needed so soon.

The ground was rising. At the top Zaister paused. A fence of trees grew along the ridge, affording concealment. Zaister gazed back towards the river. To begin with, he saw nothing mobile. Then he did see something. The hunt was almost too small to make out, unless he had known. But he did know. And they were covering ground fast, the hounds excited.

Frenziedly, Zaister looked the other way, the other side of the ridge where the slope descended steeply. It was like the answer to a prayer. A stone track had been laid over the ridge beside the trees, and a subsidiary track angled off from it, down the slope and away across the heath. About half a mile along the track was a group of ramshackle buildings. Dekteon's memory told Zaister this alien object would be a farm, but obviously in poor condition. Smoke was rising from a chimney, but beyond the main dwelling, the barns looked deserted.

Zaister, in angry fear, without ready magic, devised a hurried plan. He caught the Pallid by its arm.

'Take the chest that way. Keep to the track. Go past the house to the other buildings. Hide the chest in one of the upper storeys. Then come back for me. Run!'

The Pallid floundered quickly on, and blundered down the slope away from the ridge towards the farm.

Keeping to the stone track, it left no footprint. Despite its load and its ungainliness, it moved quite quickly. Ten minutes to reach the farm, three to stow the chest – unless it met someone, don't think of that – six minutes back up the slope, unencumbered. Then the second descent, carrying Zaister. Zaister was lighter than the chest. Eight minutes for the descent, two minutes to reach the hiding place and get into it. Twenty-nine minutes.

Zaister did not reckon the hunt could reach the ridge in less than thirty minutes. The earlier going had been uneven, and here and there he had made a detour which might confuse the hounds. Yes, it could be done. And if the pursuers did not catch sight of him actually running, and if neither he nor the Pallid met anyone among the barns, then the hunt might well give up again. There would be no footprint and no scent trail, with the odourless Pallid bearing him above ground level. Besides, there was the track that ran along the top of the ridge by the trees. At a loss, they could decide to try for him that way.

Pleased at his intelligence, but shivering, Zaister leaned on a tree trunk. He watched the Pallid dwindling on one side of the slope, the tiny dogs and horses and men getting larger on the other.

The dogs milled, and veered aside into a stand of trees. Their voices came sharper now, but only when the wind brought them. That was the spot where Zaister had sampled the berries. The dogs scrambled through a thicket, losing time. The other side of the slope, the Pallid was much smaller. There was a low wall about the farm outbuildings. Just as the dogs tumbled back on to the main trail, the Pallid clambered up on the wall and dropped over the far side out of sight.

Zaister shook. His eyes smarted. It was unjust; he had thought himself safe from horror. He gazed at the dogs. They seemed to be gaining more rapidly than before, and frantically he swung round to scan the farm. Nothing moved. How much time had gone by? Why did the Pallid not come out? Sun! He should have left the chest. But no, he could not. The chest held the instruments of his sorcery, the means to rebuild his life. He *needed* the chest.

Clear as a knife slicing butter, the baying of the hounds cut the air.

'Oh, Sun, help me . . .' Zaister said.

Should he start down the track? No, he could go no farther. The dogs must lose his scent, here at the intersection, or he had no chance.

He could see the various colours of the pack now, and the horses. A man in a blue cloak rode before the rest.

Where was the Pallid?

Suddenly the Pallid appeared. It leapt on to the track.

It would take the Pallid six minutes to reach him, eight minutes to return with him. Two minutes to hide.

The Pallid was running fast. Yet gaining ground so slowly. Zaister could see the colours of the ears of the hounds. He shut his eyes and tears slid under the lids.

The Pallid burst on to the ridge.

'Carry me,' Zaister said. He scarcely knew, any more, what he said. The Pallid raised him effortlessly, shoulder high. As a child, Zaister had made Pallids carry him about the Sun's House. 'Back the same way,' Zaister said. The Pallid sprang round and began its second dash for the farm.

The hunt was at the bottom of the incline, where Zaister had sat beneath the tree. A rabbit started from the grass, confusing the dogs for a few moments.

'You met no one,' Zaister said.

The Pallid said, unhumanly not panting as it ran, 'A man in the barn.'

Zaister's vision blackened, then cleared.

'Hurry!' he whispered uselessly. The Pallid was pounding along the track at its top speed. At every third or fourth racing step, he heard that grinding noise in its machinery. Suppose the Pallid broke down, here on the track, in full view of the ridge? Suppose sorcery could not get it moving again?

The galloping motion sickened him. He felt himself slipping into faintness and somehow dragged himself back. Dekteon's strong body, not given to fainting, helped him to regain control.

He looked over his shoulder.

The hunt had not yet crested the ridge.

The Pallid bounded forward. The farmhouse, a hovel, stood some yards off from the track, but the low wall of the outbuildings rose beside it. The wall came nearer. There was no one on the ridge.

They reached the wall.

The Pallid assisted Zaister to the top. Zaister dropped over the other side. His legs were fluid. The Pallid dropped down beside him.

They were out of sight of the ridge.

'To the barn now, where you put the chest.'

The Pallid trotted ahead of him. Zaister stared around, terrified they would come on the man the Pallid had reported seeing. Perhaps the man had not seen the Pallid?

Nothing stirred in the yard. Two dilapidated immobile pigeons peered from a creaky cot, and somewhere a goat bleated. The Pallid went into the nearer of two barns. A ladder stretched up into a hayloft without hay. Mice skittered. The Pallid climbed the ladder. A couple of rungs were freshly snapped, probably by the Pallid's previous ascent with the heavy chest. Zaister started to climb.

Far off, yet unmistakable, Zaister heard the whining ululation of hounds cheated of their trail.

He leaned his forehead on a rung of the ladder above him.

Below, a slurred gutteral voice said:

'Here, you. What're you doing in my barn?'

TEN

Shelter

Suspended on the ladder, his head swimming, Zaister turned to face the owner of the voice.

Almost at once, he was reassured. The man was young, oafish and poverty-stricken. He looked as badly-off as the human slaves Zaister had seen through the Vision Crystal, on Fren's estate; probably worse off. Certainly far worse than the lowest class of landsman in Zaister's world. Greasy brown hair, watery blue eyes and black teeth completed the unwholesome picture.

Zaister, steady now, jumped from the ladder and confronted the man, and Zaister was a good half foot taller.

'I beg your pardon for the intrusion,' Zaister said, casually.

'Uh?' queried the man.

'For entering your barn without your permission.'

'Uh,' said the man. He studied Zaister, pop-eyed at the rich, if slightly muddy, clothing, the princely look of the stranger, his bright hair. 'Not a robber, plainly,' said the man. 'Nothing worth robbing, not here. And you a lord. Plainly.'

'You're very observant, my friend,' Zaister said.

The hounds had stopped howling. Which direction had they gone? As long as they didn't come this way. At least, not for a minute or two.

The man seemed pleased to be called observant.

'Heard dogs,' he said. 'I says to Esik, that's dogs, I says.'

'Indeed.'

'Yes. I went to look, and I see a fellow run in my barn with a box on his back. Who's that? I says to myself. Then out he runs again, not a word, mind you, and off up the hill. I go to look, I do. Seeing as how it's my barn he's put his old box in. I go to look at the box.'

Zaister did not like the sound of this.

'Well?'

'Up there it is,' the man told Zaister. 'Can't open it, can I?'

'Can't you?' said Zaister, anger, relief and slight fear mingling.

'No,' said the man. 'It's yours, plainly.'

'Yes. And the fellow you saw is my servant.'

'Ah,' said the man. His watery eyes narrowed. 'Dogs after you, perhaps? Uh? Uh?'

Zaister opened his hand before the man's face, and the man gaped at the hand. Zaister forced himself to concentrate. This must work, or there could be trouble. A spiral of whirling sparks seemed to form on Zaister's palm and the man jumped, but Zaister spoke three quiet words and the man subsided. His eyes, fixed on the sparks, glazed.

119

'I am known to you,' Zaister said softly. 'I am a lord, a traveller. I have been this way before and accepted your shelter. If any come asking, you will not tell them I am here. It is our secret, which you are proud to be entrusted with. Repeat what I have said.'

The man gabbled the sentences over to him. The sparks died on Zaister's palm. Zaister was trembling again. It had been so hard to perform this simple act of mesmerism. Fatigue, perhaps. Yes, it must be that.

The man blinked. He smiled deference and black teeth at Zaister.

'Come, sir lord,' he said, 'you must be hungry. Are you hungry, sir lord?'

Zaister called up the ladder for the Pallid to bring the chest. The Pallid emerged, the chest on its back, and came down the ladder.

'Strong, plainly,' said the man. He grinned and conducted them ceremoniously out of the barn and across the yard to the hovel-farm.

The rafters of the farm were so low Zaister had to duck. Beneath them was a big space which seemed to serve as kitchen, workshop, bedchamber and byre, decorated in tones of light mud and darker mud. A muddy fire smeared the central hearth. The chimney above it was filthy, and smoked. Three or four skinny goats were tethered at one end of the room on some straw. A dog sprawled close to the fire, and another man sprawled near the dog, on a heap of rugs. There was little furniture. A cauldron with something cooking in it hung above the hearth from the chimney hook.

The room smelled of smoke, goat, dog and dirt.

Zaister, almost retching, tried to ignore the smell. From the yard, he had seen the ridge and the slope were empty of the hunt. Still, he had best stay in hiding for a while, and this ghastly hole was a hiding place.

The other man, Esik, he did not bother to work magic on. As the first man explained in detail, Esik was dumb and witless. To be sure, he looked it. The first man said Zaister should call *him* Ear – on account of the missing one, didn't sir lord remember from his last visit?

The Pallid set the chest by the hearth, the other side from the goats and the dog and Esik. Zaister sat on the chest, and the Pallid crouched by it.

Ear ladled something out of the cauldron and brought it to Zaister in a clay bowl. He asked if the servant would have any; Zaister said the servant would not. (A Pallid, naturally, had no need of food.) Ear seemed perturbed. He told Zaister his servant would get sickly if he didn't eat. Look at him now, pale as a clean sheet. Zaister wondered when, if ever, Ear had seen a clean sheet. He tried to chew and swallow what was in the bowl. It was just palatable. He managed to get some down, and keep it there.

'Yes, it's a fine old box, that,' Ear mused at the chest. 'Isn't it a fine old box, Esik, uh?'

Esik grunted.

Zaister set his food bowl, two thirds full, on the floor. The dog immediately rose and pounced on the bowl, overturning it. The dog slurped up the food. Ear took no notice.

'Yes, a fine old box, that is. Will you be staying long,

sir lord?' he added graciously to Zaister. 'There's the room upstairs you could have. Old Rewa won't mind.'

Zaister wondered if the room upstairs might be worse than this, or better. The very fact that Old Rewa, whoever he was, had a separate room, pointed to a fastidious desire to keep clear of the goats and other inhabitants of the kitchen area.

Zaister was exhausted, but wary. In his own world, as Sun's Son, he had been used to instant respect, to adoration and a willingness to serve him on the part of the men he met. Here things were different. He should be careful, despite the mesmerism of Ear. Where were the hounds now?

The dog, having finished Zaister's meal, began its toilet. It scratched itself vigorously and repeatedly, using alternate back legs.

'That's nice embroidery, that is,' Ear said, 'on the lord's tunic. Isn't it, Esik?' Esik grunted. 'Nice. Gold thread. Noticed it at once. I expect the lord's got a lot of tunics like those, I says to myself. In that box of his.'

Ear's mounting interest in the chest alarmed Zaister. But he felt there was nothing he could do.

'There's a town near here,' Zaister said, 'south-wards. Am I correct?'

'Uh? A town? Oh, yes. Meaning to travel on that way, sir lord? No, it's not a nice place. Too many robbers and snatchpurses, see that box of yours, they would, and you'd get no peace.'

'Apparently I'm to get no peace from you, either,' Zaister said. 'All the chest contains are certain personal items, of no interest to you.'

'Ah, but I'm very interested, sir lord. Truly I am. Plainly, it's an interesting old box, that is.'

Zaister gathered himself. He realized that what bothered him about these men, really bothered him, was that they were not like the men of his own world. Not only in their attitude to him, but in their whole demeanour. Even filthy Ear swaggered. Dekteon had had a sort of swagger, too. Pride in their manhood, as the women of Zaister's world were proud.

The door of the farm crashed open.

Zaister's heart stopped, then started up at a canter.

'Hallo, Rewa,' bawled Ear.

Rewa was a fat hideous woman. Her hair was the same greasy brown as that of Ear and Esik. But she had been to market to sell a goat, and had put on her best, which was a ragged stenchful dress, in colour bright red.

Zaister was appalled. Even though he knew there was no colour taboo in this world, to see a woman clad in red, and such a vivid red, shocked him. That Rewa was a woman was shock enough. Zaister was afraid of women. Like all the males of his world, he had been trained from earliest boyhood to fear them, reverence them, do what they ordered. And while he knew that here it was different, he could not shake a lifetime's training from him.

Rewa glared at Zaister, and he cowered.

'Who's that?'

'It's a lord, Rewa. He's been here before.'

'He has not!' cried Rewa forcefully.

'Yes he has, Rewa. I've offered him shelter, and he's

stayed.' Ear remained stubbornly obedient to his mesmerism. 'We're to tell no one he's here.'

'You!' Rewa shouted at Zaister. 'Who are you?'

Zaister got to his feet. He would not dare to mesmerise a woman. He could not.

'I – I am who he says.'

'What's your name?'

'Zaister.'

'I heard there were dogs out,' Rewa said, 'looking for a red-haired man.'

Zaister turned sick again.

'Lady,' he began.

'Lady, is it?' Rewa laughed. 'No, you needn't fret. We're no great lovers of law and order. So long as you pay your way, you can hide up here and welcome.' And she smiled at him. She, too, had black teeth, but because she was a woman, and seemed prepared to befriend him, Zaister smiled back. He tried to charm her, get round her with the smile. He had sometimes got round the Daughters of Night with his smile. Sometimes.

'I'm most grateful, lady.'

'Good. Then you'll pay well. That box there, you've got money in it, I'll bet. Stolen, perhaps. Let's see.'

Zaister shrank.

'I – there's nothing in the chest. A few clothes—'

'Open it,' Rewa bawled, no longer friendly.

She was a woman. He could not fight her. Cold sweat broke on his forehead. He was trembling so much he could hardly fit his palm and fingers inside the handprint he'd earlier matched to Dekteon's. One ploy was left. He muttered as he lifted the lid. A spell of illusion was bound into the fabric of the chest, just as a similar spell had been bound into his room in the duplicate tower of the between-place. It would make the room, or the chest, appear empty. He needed only to speak the right words to activate it. He could say he'd been robbed already.

But something strange happened. Zaister spoke the words of the spell, but he said them wrongly. They came out jumbled, mispronounced. He tried to correct himself, but it was too late. The woman was already beside him, staring in, plunging her hands among the caskets and inner compartments of the chest.

The spell had not been activated. She would see everything as it really was, alien, peculiar, *rich*.

'Why, there's gold here,' Rewa said. She picked up the gold cup and clamped her foul teeth in the stem to test it. 'Real gold!'

'Please,' Zaister faltered.

Ear, thrusting forward, shovelled Zaister aside. Esik, the witless one, blundered up, too. He seized from the chest a weird-shaped instrument of sorcery. Zaister shouted at his Pallid. The Pallid did not move.

Dribbling and soundlessly chuckling, Esik flung the instrument at Zaister. Zaister jerked involuntarily backward. His skull crashed against one of the low rafters.

As he fell in a blur of darkness, Zaister heard Ear, very far off, saying to Rewa, 'He tried some game on me, out in the barn. Little lights in his hand. He told me I knew him, and to keep quiet he was here. I acted up. Saw the quack-doctor do something like it once, before he pulled some poor devil's tooth out. Said it'd stop him feeling the pain, he did. But it never. Didn't work with me, either. Ear, I says to myself, we've got a funny one here, I says. Plainly.'

'Izvire,' Zaister groaned. And came to.

His head rang with nauseous pain. He could not for a minute recall where he was. He wished Izvire would answer his pleading cry. He needed her. Then he realized she was in another world. He recollected everything.

He tried to get up, but slumped back. The pain in his head, where it had struck the rafter, exploded, then subsided to a hot insistent ache.

As he lay there, helpless, terrified and alone, Zaister felt someone watching him. He rolled his eyes, searching. He was in the 'room upstairs', Rewa's chamber. It was as filthy and unpleasant as the area below. He had been cast on a large lumpy bed. There was no window. A candle, shielded by grimy glass, burned on an iron spike protruding from the wall. In the flickering twilight, Zaister could see no one was with him, no one watched. The sensation faded.

There were boots on the stairs. Ear came in. He was draped in a cloak of yellow velvet. On his shoulders rested a collar of gold set with polished rubies. He swept a bow to Zaister.

'Better now, sir lord? We're having something of a celebration, Rewa, Esik and me. And I says to Rewa, I says, maybe the lord's feeling better and 'ud like to join in the fun, uh?'

Zaister became aware of a mindless din going on below. The woman was singing and laughing raucously.

Even the dumb man was making a kind of awful festive noise.

'My servant . . .' Zaister croaked.

'Oh, he's not well,' Ear said. 'Dead, or having a fit. You plainly should've fed him better, sir lord.'

Zaister remembered how he had shouted at the Pallid and it had not moved. The mechanism had finally failed, then. He would somehow have to . . . But his sorcerous instruments would be ruined by now. These people would have seen to that. As for his spells . . . What was the matter with him? Obviously, Ear had not been mesmerised after all. Or, if he had, it had not lasted. And then the spell with the chest . . . Zaister attempted to think what the spell should be. He could not.

The solution came sudden, and unbelievable. Zaister reared up again, despite the hurt to his head. For a moment he sat, mouthing at Ear, but not seeing him. Then he turned and ran his finger through the dust on the rotten plaster wall.

Ear was curious. It almost looked as if the mad, rich, stupid stranger were trying to write something in the dust. Ear could not read or write. Neither, apparently, could the stranger. He made faltering marks in the dust, then smoothed them and began again, more nervously, in another spot. Presently he ran out of dust.

Zaister screamed. He covered his head with his arms and wept.

Ear shrugged, and went downstairs.

Rewa and the idiot were drunk on some sour wine they had found in a gold flask in the box. Once or twice the three of them had robbed travellers, but never been

127

so lucky as to get a haul like this. And there was a bonus, too, as Rewa shortly pointed out.

The anaemic bald servant lay in the corner. He seemed to be unconscious. Tomorrow, if he didn't get better or wake up, Ear would get Esik to dig a grave and dump the servant in it.

Upstairs, Ear could hear the traveller sobbing.

'A grown man, and snivelling,' Rewa said in loathing. 'He deserves what's coming to him.' Later, she went up, wrapped in new red silk, and loomed over Zaister threateningly. 'Shut your noise,' she said.

Zaister stared at her, and fell silent.

As the magic of the gold chariot had opened Zaister's physical brain to Dekteon, so the blow on the head had opened Dekteon's physical brain to Zaister, with an opposite effect.

Since he had entered Dekteon's body, Zaister had been hampered by Dekteon's brain's ignorance, without realizing it. Now that ignorance flooded Zaister's mind.

It was not that he had ceased to be a sorcerer, merely that Dekteon's lack of sorcery blotted the ability out. Dekteon could not read or write. His hand had never formed letters or words on paper, not even on a wall. Zaister, contained in Dekteon's flesh, found he had become as mentally impoverished as Dekteon had been. It was like burying a knife to its hilt in mud. The blade was still there, but you could not reach it for the mud. The mud hid the knife and made it useless.

Zaister had not known this would happen. Rather, he had counted on its not happening.

Now, the eyes of his intelligence and learning blinded,

doomed to an unknown hell, Zaister lay curled in a knot on the robber woman's bed. Afraid even to whimper.

ELEVEN

In the Dark

Two days Zaister was kept in the upstairs room. They brought him disgusting stews to eat, and left a slop bowl in the corner for his other needs. They would not let him out of the room. The dumb man kept guard on the stair.

The first day, Ear went off somewhere. At sunset of the second day he came back. Twelve men came with him. Outside, horses stamped and hounds bickered.

Ear had investigated and found the slave brand on Dekteon's body's shoulder. He had gone seeking the hunt, and brought it back with him.

Presently, Ear led three men upstairs. They crowded into the bedchamber. Two of them were retainers of Lord Fren of By-the-Lake. The other was Fren himself.

Dekteon's brain identified Fren immediately. Even Zaister had seen him through the Vision Crystal.

Fren wore a blue cloak, the same cloak he had worn on the hunting. It was travel-stained. He had been determined to catch his troublesome red slave. Now he had. Fren's little soft mouth smiled, as Dekteon had seen it smile hundreds of times. Zaister could only lie on the bed, part mad with his despair and fear, seeing it too.

'Well,' Fren said, 'I hope you enjoyed your bit of liberty, Red. You know where you're going now, don't you? No, not hanging. Hanging's too quick. A slower death in the mines for you, and money for your master who's had such poor wear out of you.'

Ear made an ingratiating noise. Fren glanced at one of his men. 'Pay the fellow what I agreed.' The man slung a bag of coins at Ear. A couple of Fren's guard had squeezed into the room by now. They pulled Zaister off the bed, and hustled him down the stair.

In the main area, the robber woman, the idiot, the dog and the goats watched the proceedings with great interest. Zaister's broken Pallid was gone. Lord Fren had said he had no interest in a dead white-faced runaway. It was just the red one he wanted. He had paid well. Rewa curtsied to Fren when he went out. She had had Esik drag the box of good things into one of the barns. Fren had not mentioned being robbed of valuables. Nobody had. So no need to tell about the box.

In the yard, one of the guards kicked Zaister to his knees. The other bound his hands behind him to an iron pole. Then they both kicked him to his feet again.

Hounds, horses and men rode off into the gathering dusk.

Ear was throwing Fren's gold pieces about. Rewa stopped him. She made him take Esik and two spades, and go out and dig a grave behind the woodstore for the body of the pale servant which they had hidden there.

When she heard the spades clanking on the hard earth, Rewa sat down to count the coins.

Thoroughly demoralized, at the brink of his sanity, Zaister hardly knew what was happening to him. He was aware of discomfort and pain as he was goaded along among the horses, compelled to keep up with a swift trot. His hands and arms hurt excrutiatingly, bound as they were. Soon the pain spread to his shoulders and chest. Once he fell down, losing consciousness. But they slapped him alert, and forced him on. Dekteon's strong body survived. Zaister's mind started to crumble into darkness.

He began to worry less about his fate and what had happened to him than about the iron pole he was bound to. Iron and silver were the women's metals. The more pliable bronze and gold were a man's. He was breaking the taboo.

After a night's camp, Fren's party struck back the way first Dekteon, and then Zaister in Dekteon's flesh, had run. They re-crossed the river, then turned westwards. At sunset Fren ordered a second camp. The next morning Fren had got bored. He meant to return home, and gave the matter of selling the slave into the hands of his retainers. Before he rode off with half the men, he came and looked at Zaister, tethered to a tree.

'Copper hair in the copper mines,' said Fren. He laughed at his joke. 'That'll teach you to muck about with my horses.'

When Fren was gone, the men moved more slowly. Still, by noon they had reached a town. Three guard and one of the retainers took Zaister into the yard of an ugly building. Some transaction was carried out. A tall man came and examined Zaister; that was, Dekteon's body. He squinted at the teeth and kneaded the muscles. He fingered the slave brand on Dekteon's body's shoulder – the bar and wings, which meant *This bird cannot fly*.

'Flown quite a way though, ain't ya?' said the man.

Zaister was unbound from the pole. Instead, his legs were chained together at the ankle so he could not walk, and could barely stand. A cart came into the yard, with six outriders jogging behind.

In the cart was a group of men. They were unkempt and wild-eyed. Their feet were chained together and, in turn, the short chains were bolted to the cart's side.

'Into the Happy-Wagon with you,' said the tall man. With the aid of one of Fren's guards, he shoved Zaister up into the cart. Zaister's chain was bolted to the side of the cart. Like the other men, he was now trapped until someone should release him.

The other captives stared at him. There was neither compassion nor dislike in their looks. They seemed to have slipped beyond humanity.

The driver of the cart, whom Zaister had not noticed, cracked a whip over the four-horse team. They began to move. The outriders spurred up and fell in behind.

Fren's retainer was drinking wine with a fat man who had emerged from the building.

The cart went through the town. People pointed at the cart, and the men in it. A woman called a curse, either at the captives or at those who bore them to the mines. Beyond the town gates, the road became rough. The chained men, who had been standing, gradually tumbled down like ungainly toys. The outriders laughed.

The man next to Zaister began to shout and swear, pummelling the sides of the cart with his fists. No one paid any attention. Eventually he stopped.

The journey took a little over three days.

Each sundown, or thereabouts, the cart would halt at a way-station. Then the captive men were unchained from the cart and allowed to hobble about in their leg chains. Later, they were fed on rough bread and meat bones and given water. The outriders and cart driver could sleep inside the station, and the horses were stabled. The captives lay in an open yard, and the second night it rained. Occasionally during the day, as the cart made on westwards, the driver and outriders would pause for a rest, or to visit a wineshop on the road. Then the captives were simply left in the cart. Sometimes children came up and stared at them and threw things, till an outrider heard and ran from the inn to chase them off.

The land altered. Hilly and wooded before, it now ascended into rocky uplands. Some squat cliffs crouched in the distance. Leaves were falling from all the trees they passed. At night, a yellow quarter moon appeared.

Zaister feared the moon, but he dared not express his fear. The other men seemed not to see it. But Zaister knew it was watching him. He could feel its scrutiny.

They came to the mines suddenly in the icy morning. A gateway led through a wall of sheer rock. The gate was manned, and buildings clustered nearby. Beyond the wall, there opened out a kind of nightmare-ish desert landscape. The rock was a great basin, high cliffs all round. Three quarters of the cliff had been chiselled and battered into terraces which cascaded away into pits and apparently haphazard craters. Wooden towers marched across this scene, and figures scrambled up and down the terraces. Fires burned here and there, the rock was grey and naked otherwise, although blackened in places. Rubble rose in small mountains. Wooden bridges ran between the terraces at various junctures, and the cart turned on to one of these which led straight to the far side of the rock basin. The air smelled unpleasant, and resounded with metallic noise.

The wooden bridge ran through the far side of the rock cliff and came out in another basin. A track, scattered alongside by huts and more wooden towers, went up to a high plateau. There were black entrances to be seen in the cliff behind the plateau.

The cart stopped at the end of the bridge, where the track started. A group of leather and fur clad men came out of one of the larger huts.

Zaister and the other captives were unchained from the cart for the last time.

Bread and beer was brought. Lightheaded from hunger and wretchedness, the captives became quickly drunk. They were taken to a room in the large hut and branded with the branch-like mark of the mine. Few escaped from that place, but it had been known. The overseers took no chances.

Zaister, seeing the brand sear the flesh of the other

135

men, knew he would scream when it touched him. He screamed.

An overseer ordered a group of ten men through one of the black doorways cut in the cliff. Torches flared in the walls of the cliff. A short way along, the men were pushed into a wooden cage-like contraption. The cage, with the men in it, was lowered by a creaking windlass into the gut of the mine.

Zaister, one of the ten, had entered a stage of such dazed horror it had not seemed possible it could increase. Yet, falling into the black below, his terror reached so great a pitch that he sprawled face downwards in the cage.

His companions cursed, but otherwise ignored him.

The dark represented an ultimate Night to Zaister. A taboo. It was not alleviated by the dim glare which gradually appeared from the bottom of the shaft. The cage jarred on a rock floor and stopped. The overseer, who had ridden with them, sent the men out of the cage. He uncurled his whip and slashed at Zaister.

'No,' Zaister said.

'Yes,' said the overseer. He dragged and thrust Zaister from the cage. 'Just you see: you'll get to like it soon.'

One of the other men laughed bitterly.

The rock passage led into a larger hollow chamber which was hot and oppressive, being poorly ventilated. Wick lamps burned in the niches of weirdly sculpted rock pillars, and wooden posts of various types supported the low ceiling where the pillars did not. Men toiled like weary automata. Picks swung up and bit at the rock and swung down. A line of slaves staggered by, large baskets of ore material tied on their backs. Somewhere, a dull rumble made the cavern vibrate. A shower of particles fell from the ceiling. The men brushed them off their heads and shoulders uninterestedly and went on chipping at the copper veins.

'You and you,' the overseer said, 'and you.' This time he meant Zaister. He took them through the cavern, into another rock passage, unlighted. Zaister moaned in the blackness. They came on to a wooden bridge suspended over black nothing. But a second cavern opened at the far end, and there, light jumped viciously.

The overseer spoke to another.

'The red one, he's dark-shy. Better keep him down till he gets used to it. No going up to sleep.'

The light came from a trough of fire against the cavern's back. Although already it was blazing fiercely, men were throwing on fresh armfuls of logs. Zaister watched them with the non-comprehension of a creature trapped by a bad dream.

The new overseer slapped Zaister across the head to get his attention. 'Fire-setting for you.'

Zaister was whipped forward with the rest. A load of wood, the rough sections of trees, filled his arms. Borne with the log-gang to the edge of the trough, he, too, let go his burden into the fire.

The heat was frightful. The rock blistered and glowed menacingly. The tongues of flame leaped up. It was difficult to breathe, for there was a shortage of the hot, foul-smelling air.

Someone shouted.

The log-gang scattered. Zaister was pulled with them. A beam swung by overhead, manned from a ledge above by a crew of blackened slaves. Zaister was not far enough away when the ready-punctured sack of water hit the red-hot face of the rock.

Scalding steam filled the cavern. The fire-setting gangs, sheltering where they could, coughed, spat and yelped. The mark of a fire-setter was his scar tissue and his boiled skin.

The rock-face cracked. Shards showered outwards, then blocks tumbled from it among the smouldering ash of the fire trough.

The gangs of men crawled forward to retrieve the broken particles of copper ore.

They crawled over Zaister.

An overseer presently saw him and rolled him aside, mouthing obscenities. Not badly scalded, no worse than several men on their feet and still labouring, Zaister lay among the rubble, wide-eyed.

The scene was very clear. The exhausted yet perpetual movement of the work-gangs. The part-extinguished fire. Zaister, lying in the rubble.

Too clear.

It was quite simple for Dekteon to recall that this could so easily have been his own condition. The hunt, the betrayal, the journey to the mines, and the final sentence of slow death which the mines meant.

Dekteon closed his eyes a moment. He leant his forehead on the cool surface of the amber Vision Crystal in which the image of the mine and of Zaister were still to be seen.

It had not been difficult to find Zaister. Zaister and Dekteon were parallels, twins. As Zaister had quickly traced Dekteon by use of his spells and the sorcerous Crystal, so Dekteon, as soon as he had understood Zaister's magic, had been able to trace Zaister as quickly. The Crystal was an instrument that conducted and enforced the sorcerer's will. Generally it was used to relay to him scenes of distant places, and was activated by pressing a series of sensitive points in the column beneath it. When it was active, the sorcerer concentrated his mind upon it, until he summoned in its shadowy surface a view of the area or person he sought. The more cunning and skilful the sorcerer, the more he might then achieve by use of magic and illusion worked through the Crystal. Zaister was exceptionally cunning and skilful. First, he had created a Vortex Gate and, by means of it, sent the non-human Pallid through into an alternate world. Next, he had wrought an illusion on the Pallid, turning it into the appearance of an old slave, who would fool and influence Dekteon. And the illusion had convinced not merely Dekteon himself, but others of Fren's household who saw the Pallid. Dekteon had 'remembered' doing these things, or rather Zaister doing them, once Zaister's brain became open to him.

What had made Dekteon trace Zaister in the Crystal he was less sure of. Perhaps only a sort of guilt. He had spent two days and nights of happiness with Zaister's wife. Possibly he wanted to salve his conscience by seeing Zaister free in the other world; to recall that Zaister had callously sentenced Dekteon to death in this one. But when he found Zaister, Dekteon recognised at once the impending disaster. Zaister's mind was being fogged by Dekteon's ignorance, as Dekteon's had been illuminated by Zaister's knowledge. More, Zaister had inherited Dekteon's dangers, as Dekteon had been delivered to his own.

It had been three hours before dawn, this second night in Zaister's world, that Dekteon had left Izvire sleeping, and gone back to the Sun's House and into the secret room of the tower. He had activated the Crystal and searched for Zaister. Soon enough he saw him.

Zaister had passed through a second Vortex Gate at the same instant Dekteon had been propelled through his. That had to be. But once in Dekteon's world and Dekteon's body, Zaister had idled. He had lazed in a cave a day and a night, while the Pallid brought through the chest of valuables from the between-place. Zaister had made plans in the cave. He had meant to make a good life for himself in his new home.

But the plans were haphazard and inadequate, and had clearly failed.

Dekteon observed Zaister. He took in the bedroom of a hovel. He registered the facts of Zaister's alarm and pain. Then the man Ear had entered. Dekteon had pieced events together swiftly – Zaister helpless among robbers who coveted the chest of gold and silk. The damaged Pallid which could no longer aid Zaister. Imminent betrayal.

Then he witnessed Zaister's terrible realization that his powers had been obscured. He watched Zaister try to write. He watched Zaister scream and weep.

Dekteon was aware it might have been a moment of triumph: Zaister, who had condemned him to a dreadful destiny, condemned to one equally dreadful. Or worse.

But Dekteon felt no triumph. He had become too much identified with Zaister not to experience discomfort and compassion for the man who had stolen his body and his life with such dire results.

If he could have helped Zaister he would have done. But he could think of no solution. And this filled him with frustration, almost anguish.

And then something else struck him, and chilled him through. Zaister's physical form could not pass into Dekteon's world any more than Dekteon's could pass into Zaister's. An exchange of bodies had been effected as both simultaneously entered the Vortex Gates. Now, Dekteon occupied Zaister's body. If Zaister died, which meant that Dekteon's body would die – Dekteon could never regain that body. And therefore could never regain his own world.

It was odd. Dekteon had not really thought of an escape back to earthlands until now, when he saw the chance slipping away. Somehow, the notion had been growing that he could outwit the Daughters of Night on their own ground, rather than run from them. Even so, the idea that the gate to his earth might be shut forever appalled him.

Abruptly, everything which had been hazed-over by his time with Izvire took on a sharp desperate urgency.

Later, Dekteon made himself leave the tower. He did

not want the priestesses to think he had fled to the shadow-place, as they termed it, again. Izvire met him smiling, but he was constrained. Presently, her smile died and her manner altered. He could not help wounding her or angering her. He was preoccupied.

In the days which followed, Dekteon had gone often to the tower, activated the Vision Crystal. He saw Fren come smiling, and Zaister taken. He glimpsed Esik and Ear burying the Pallid behind the woodstore. He viewed Zaister's journey west.

At length Dekteon beheld the insides of the mine, Zaister whimpering with fear of the dark, the scalding steam. Zaister lying in the rubble.

Dekteon must save Zaister, because otherwise he would lose, literally, his own self.

And yet, he could think of no solution.

And, intelligent magician that he now was, he could think of no solution to that other small problem of his, the sacrifice. He felt he could defeat the women, evade death. But how?

It looked very much after all as if Zaister would die, and so would he.

The night after Zaister's scalding, after Dekteon had seen him whipped back into blank-eyed action, Dekteon had a dream.

He dreamed he had got free of the women. But he was still running from them across the alien landscape, which now seemed as unnatural as when he had first come there.

Great winds howled by. The earth quivered and

sometimes pitched him over. The sun shone, but it was black.

Of course. He had evaded death. Kyrast had told him if the Sun consort did not die at the allotted time, all these disasters would follow. He hadn't believed her then, but it was apparently true.

Here and there, groups of people stood staring with huge eyes. They were chained together at the ankles, and some carried picks with which they swung at the darkness, trying to dismantle it.

Dekteon was not afraid in the dream, only depressed.

Then he met the old slave from Fren's Shore House at By-the-Lake. The old slave who had really been a Pallid under illusion.

And the slave said: 'The answer is here.'

And Dekteon woke, knowing it was.

TWELVE

Sorcery in the Dark

In the hovel-farm by the stone track, three persons were
snoring: downstairs, Esik and Ear round the remains of
a jug of ale; upstairs, Rewa. A new canopy overhung her
bed: a red silk cloak.

Awake, she had been impatient with the two men. It
had come to blows. It was time they took the cart, she
said, and got some of the smaller items from the chest
to the crooked dealer in town. But Ear, and that idiot,
taking Ear's lead, preferred to buy liquor at the tavern,
bring it home and become drunk. Rewa also had
become drunk, despite her annoyance.

The snores rattled through the hovel.

Suddenly, there came, from the silence beyond the
farm, a loud unlikely noise.

Rewa's snores at least cut off. She sat up, instantly and
hideously alert. Her vigilance was not unrewarded. The
sound came again. It was like – like what? – a pile of
stones and loose soil tumbling on to a hard surface. It
seemed to come from some part of the yard.

Rewa rose and pulled a dirty blanket round her. In

144

the windowless dark, she found and struck a flint. A flame bobbed on the shielded candle, and she yanked it, complete with its rusty spike, from the wall, and went heavily down the stairs. Below, she gave Ear a kick to rouse him, but he was too far gone. She pulled the dog up instead. Taking the meat knife in her other hand, she flung open the door into the yard.

The moon had set, and the stars showed the yard indistinctly. Nothing was to be seen, but even as she stood there, Rewa heard a fresh noise. A crash, followed by the rolling clatter of logs of wood on the move.

So. The villain was in the woodstore. Rewa grunted with menacing contempt. Probably Ear had prattled about their box at the tavern. Now some wretch had come to rob them of their rightful possessions.

Rewa was brave. At least, she was thick-witted enough to be able to ignore personal danger to a great extent.

She trampled into the yard, candle and knife to hand, the dog at her heels, growling softly.

'Clear off!' she bellowed into the night. 'Or come and see *me*. I'm waiting!'

Rewa had a certain reputation. Once or twice thieves had run for the heath at her cry. Not, however, this time.

Slightly perturbed, Rewa heard steps coming her way from the direction of the nearer barn. She hefted the knife more firmly. The steps, though, were very slow and faltering. Perhaps the devil was tipsy. She raised her candle high. Then it fell out of her hand.

Around the corner of the barn, stumbling and dragging his feet and covered with bits of earth from his uprooted grave, came the white-faced corpse of the man Ear and Esik had buried more than six days ago.

Rewa would have screamed, but the scream stuck. Instead, on a reflex, she flung the knife right at him.

The knife hit the man full in the chest, and went in. And stayed in. But there was no blood, and the man kept on walking right towards her, with his shuffling awkward gait. And his eyes glowed like phosphorus.

Rewa managed to scream. She dashed round and pelted into the farm, slamming the door on the dog. The dog, unafraid, ambled up to the walking corpse. It sniffed at the scentless legs, and then trotted away into the night, remembering dog business of its own.

Rewa shook Ear, screeching at him. Ear came to blearily. Rewa contrived to push the large cauldron against the boltless door. There was no other furniture to make a barricade, except the stolen chest, which was too heavy for her to shift. And the cauldron did no good.

As Ear, protesting, opened both his eyes at once, he was greeted by the sight of the door flying open and the revived corpse blundering in.

Ear and Rewa screamed in harmony.

The corpse advanced into the room and straight to the chest. On the way it removed the knife from its heart, and laid it neatly on the floor.

'Oh, merciful God – oh!' babbled Rewa. She and Ear crowded into the goats' end of the room. The goats set up a mournful bleating, not afraid, but prepared to join in for form's sake.

The corpse slowly and carefully opened the chest. It

fished about inside. Presently it produced a strange instrument of bronze and held it up, as if for someone to see. Then it discarded the implement, and held up another. This happened several times. Rewa and Ear were reduced to squeaking prayers.

At last the corpse seemed to find what it wanted. It swivelled the instrument around and inserted it in its own abdomen.

Esik awoke. His reaction was unoriginal. He quickly plunged to join the others in the corner.

The three of them gibbered and moaned as the bronze instrument twirled off the belly of the corpse.

Inside the belly was a complicated arrangement of wheels, spokes, grooves and tubes. As the trio watched, a pale red disc began to glow there, and sparks flew.

They were presently not the only things to fly.

Early travellers on the town road might have discerned three part-dressed howling people running for their lives. Half a mile behind them, running more jauntily, four thin goats with mysteriously cut tethers. Two miles behind them, a puzzled, flea-ridden dog.

The Pallid, its mechanism restored, went the other way, back towards the river.

To begin with, Dekteon had considered sending another Pallid through into the other world. But it seemed unwise, since the women kept a check on the numbers of Pallids in the Sun's House, and had already noted the absence of the first. Deciding to use the original Pallid then, Dekteon had supposed it would be difficult, perhaps impossible, to work such magic through the medium of the Vision Crystal. But it was not. Though Zaister had never attempted such extreme feats, they were easy once the correct balance of concentration and determination had been established. Zaister, his powers waning, had not been able to restore the broken Pallid, but Dekteon had done it in one half of an hour; raised it from its grave, sent it into the farm and repaired it fully with one of the instruments Zaister had taken with him. Success piled on success. Exhilarated, Dekteon pushed the Pallid onward through the night of two worlds.

The Pallid ran. Over the starlit slopes and through the copses of the heath. Across the river. Westward. An hour after sunrise, a wagon went by. Dekteon made the Pallid drop from sight into a ditch, then scramble out and race on when the wagon had gone over the hill.

It had taken Fren's party almost two days to reach the western town, and a little more than three for the slave-cart to reach the mines. But the Pallid could run astonishingly fast when unburdened and in complete working order.

There was an interruption.

Another Pallid, one of the Sun's House army of 'Frens', scratched at the tower door. Izvire waited in the Great Room. Would Dekteon go riding with her? Dekteon foresaw he must show himself, refuse her in person, or she would think trouble was brewing, and he did not want that. He felt tired and slightly feverish. He had had little sleep and much to do.

Since discovering Zaister's plight, Dekteon had not bothered with his earlier games of rebellion. He decorously wore red when in the women's company; he returned Vesain, crying and reluctant, to Izvire's custody, and was polite. Izvire obviously thought his reformed behaviour due to some charm she had exercised over him, and this amused him.

Now her face was grave.

'You won't come with me,' she said, 'but you should. What are you doing, my husband, that takes you away from me so much?'

He could see the old hurt and anxiety back in her eyes. He did not like to hurt her. He wished he could tell her what he was really doing, but she would try to stop him, and her powers were not slight.

'One last magic,' he said lightly. 'It will be finished by tonight.'

'Will it? May I see it then?'

'If you like.' He could always substitute something harmless.

'Zaister—' she said. Her mouth had hardened. 'Please don't do any foolish thing.'

Foolish! he thought.

'I swear I won't,' he said.

She went away, cold and very pale.

He rushed back to the tower. He had sent the Pallid up a tree for safety. The ludicrous aspect of this made Dekteon laugh. He brought the Pallid down and set it bounding on towards the mines.

It was late in the afternoon. Only two guards stood at the Rock Gate of the mines in the biting wind. Up the slope came a man in overseer's uniform, a man they

149

knew to be a surly clod. He passed through the gate, as he always did, without a word.

The leather uniform was not real. Nor was the overseer. But it was a good likeness of him, fashioned on the Pallid by Dekteon.

The 'overseer' strutted across the first rock basin bridge, through the cliff wall, up the track of the second basin, in at the black mouth of the mine.

'Not your duty, is it, Smiler?' called the fat man in charge of the windlass gang. The nickname was greeted, as ever, by a scowl.

'Down!' the 'overseer' ordered.

They lowered him down in the cage.

'Smiler' walked through the caverns of the mine to the second windlass shaft. Here the ore was being loaded, ready to be hauled aloft. Slave after slave, bent over under the basket on his back, toiled up to the shaft entry. A load gang grabbed the material from the basket and threw it into the ore-cage. The slave rested briefly as his burden lightened, then trudged back into the depths of the mine to be loaded up once more.

The light was extremely poor here. The bulk of the wick lamps were kept to illuminate the veins. Two overseers lounged by the shaft.

'Here's Smiler,' said one. 'Sweet to see your happy face.'

The Pallid said, in an approximation of Smiler's voice, 'The red slave is wanted above.'

'Oh, that one. He'll be dead in a couple more days. The burns aren't bad. But he's gone, up there,' tapping his head. 'Won't eat. Should get the cash back from his cheating master. This sort're no good to us here.'

On cue, Zaister appeared, or rather Dekteon's body. The body looked almost dead now, staggering under the basket load. The eyes were half-shut and unseeing.

'Basket release!' shouted the overseer to whom this sort were no good. Two slaves ran to unstrap the red man from his load. He fell to his knees.

'Smiler' stepped forward, and to the astonishment of his fellow overseers, lifted the red man in his arms and carried him away.

Ten minutes later, with no hindrance, they reached the surface.

The Pallid set Zaister against the wall of rock. It was comparatively secluded here, but activity surged all about. All the less reason for this particular activity to be noticed.

The Pallid stripped Zaister's rags. It took out the salve, which had remained with it even in the grave, and applied it to the boiled and blistered skin. Almost immediately the reddened area cooled off in colour. Zaister opened his eyes.

'Master,' the Pallid said, 'Dekteon sent me.'

'Dekteon,' Zaister said. He began to cry. 'Poor Dekteon.'

'Master,' said the Pallid, 'I will give you my clothing. You will pull up the hood to hide your hair. You will be able to leave the mine, for I shall make a diversion. Beyond the gate, go east. Dekteon has made me say this.'

Zaister smiled feebly. The Pallid dressed Zaister in its own garments which had been made to resemble the overseer's. The Pallid pulled the fur hood over Zaister's head and sat him up.

'Dekteon,' Zaister said. His eyes cleared. He looked afraid.

The Pallid was altering. One illusion melted into another.

The Pallid was tanned and steam-burned. It wore rags. It had a wild look. Its hair was dark red. It was Dekteon.

Zaister tried to speak to this Dekteon. But, out of nowhere, out of the air itself, a force seemed to hit Zaister. He had to get to his feet, had to start walking. Along the rock, down the track, towards the wooden bridge . . .

Behind him came a yell.

Somehow Zaister could not look about.

Therefore he did not see the illusory Dekteon go berserk. Did not see Dekteon whirling a pick, upsetting a brazier, running, screaming. Men came from the wooden towers and huts. But this Dekteon could run faster than them all.

As Zaister walked through the rock wall and began to cross the outer rock basin towards the gate, Dekteon rushed after him, hotly pursued.

By the time Zaister was approaching the gate, commotion had broken out. Mutiny caught suddenly, like brush fire. Other slaves, inspired by the red man's crazy career, also began to strike about with their picks. A tower caught flame. The flames sprang to a wooden bridge. Smoke billowed.

Zaister was at the gate. The guards came bursting

inwards, leaving the gate open and unguarded.

Zaister did not look back. The row behind him was like an angry sea imprisoned in a cauldron.

Zaister found he was running eastwards.

About a mile from the gate, the Pallid caught him up and picked him up. The Pallid looked just like a Pallid again.

The sun was almost down, but, for Zaister, the sunset was not vivid enough, not like his own world.

Gratefully, Zaister lost consciousness.

So he did not see loom up on the nearby hill a ring of stones. Nor was he aware when the Pallid bore him into the centre of them.

It had been as simple for Dekteon to re-establish the Vortex Gate as to do everything else. Though he had not troubled to make the power-conducting stones seem old. Instead, they were fabulous smooth posts of green shining tourmaline.

The Pallid lifted Zaister into the cavity beneath the central slab, climbed in also, pulled the slab back into place above them.

The circle of stones trembled in the sunset air. And vanished.

Part Four

THIRTEEN

The Temple

The Moon Temple was white, striped by black pillars. The altar was in the shape of a horned ivory cat. Behind the altar was a completely circular door of solid silver, itself a symbol of the moon. Behind the moon-door, the secret rooms of the Temple opened into one another. One room had a ceiling painted with stars. Izvire sat there, awaiting Kyrast, her mother.

Izvire did not think of the High Priestess as a mother. From the beginning, Izvire had been reared by nurses, Kyrast a remote figure in the distance – the king. Izvire's own daughter should have been raised in the same sort of atmosphere.

Vesain sat now at Izvire's side, stiff as a post. Vesain's hair had been carefully re-dyed black. The nurse who stood in the background still bore the scratches that had marked this event. Vesain firmly grasped Zaister's gold toy bird. The mechanism which made the bird speak insults had been removed, also the mechanism which enabled the bird to fly – it was deemed too dangerous for a child to handle. However, the bird could still strut and pick about when put on the ground. Vesain slept with the bird on her pillow. She had cried when she had been returned to her nurses. Vesain said she wanted to go back to Zaister. She said it over and over. Izvire looked at Vesain surreptitiously. What will happen to my daughter, Izvire thought, when Zaister dies? She tried to ignore the clutching sensation at her own heart: What will happen to *me*?

Kyrast entered.

The nurse bowed from her corner. The child's mouth turned even further down. She gripped the toy bird angrily.

'Well,' said Kyrast. She glanced at the nurse, and pointed to the door. The nurse went quickly out. 'Well,' said Kyrast again, 'three of us together: child, woman and crone. What do you need, Izvire?'

'You can guess,' Izvire said.

'I can. A new and stronger drug to mix in his wine to stop the fear.'

'I suppose that's the answer,' said Izvire.

'Thirteen days,' said Kyrast, 'and then it's over.'

Izvire looked away. 'Don't say it.'

'Why not? It's true. Thirteen days, and then a new Sun.'

'The child,' said Izvire.

'The child will get used to it, as you will.'

Kyrast turned her milky but ruthless gaze on Vesain, who gazed ruthlessly back. As can happen, the resemblance had skipped a generation. It was the grandmother and the grandchild who were stubbornly alike; Izvire was the stranger.

'Vesain loves him,' Izvire said. 'She cares for no one *but* him.'

'And you care for him, too.'

Izvire said quietly, 'Yes. I loved him in the beginning. I love my lions in the same way that I loved him then. After that, I hated him. Now I love him again. Differently. As a man. Perhaps *I* need the drug rather than Zaister. To tell you the truth, he doesn't seem afraid. But he's spending a lot of time in the tower, as he did before. He has been using the Vision Crystal, I think, as before. For two or three days he and I were very close. Now, I don't understand him. And I don't trust him. Do you see?'

'I do,' said Kyrast. 'They all have their different moods, near the end. I'll give you something for him. But not for you. You must harden yourself and go on alone. It's the only way, my lass.'

Vesain suddenly put the gold bird on the floor. The bird began to peck about busily.

Kyrast leaned down to the child.

'Gold is not for women. It's a soft metal that melts easily. Your metal is silver, little brat.'

Vesain picked the bird up and carried it out of Kyrast's reach.

Kyrast straightened. She ignored the child and, going to the door, called the nurse back in. Then Kyrast led Izvire out of the starry room. They crossed a gallery and climbed a black marble stair. Above was a silver door with a series of handprints in the metal. Kyrast set her narrow hand in the topmost print. The door broke into two half moons, each of which slid aside into the walls.

Beyond was a chamber of sorcery. It was similar to Zaister's room in the tower. Before a window of green glass stood a Vision Crystal. It was black.

The door closed.

Izvire stared at the black Crystal on its silver stand.

She remembered how, at every full moon, she and the priestesses had come here. How the chamber had seemed to broaden and hollow out, stretching gradually into a wide luminous marble desert, empty of everything except the pictures in the Crystal, the women and their magic.

At full moon. Every full moon for almost a year, she had joined her powers with those of the priestesses. They had activated the Temple Vision Crystal, made sorcery, and searched for Zaister.

Normally, she had pitied Zaister, even been anxious for him, but never at those times of sorcery. For when the moon was full, Izvire was no longer herself, no longer in command of herself. She ceased to be a human, and became all king, all priestess and all witch. It was part of her destiny: an ancient seal laid upon the Royal Women. Izvire, remembering herself as she must have been on those nights, as she would be again, trembled.

They had located Zaister, located but not properly comprehended where he was. It was a misty, incomplete picture they received. Despite their spells, they could not reach him. And they tried to. Very hard they tried. When they eventually admitted that they were not able to break through to him, they began instead to terrorize him. The image of Kyrast's black crow projected through the Crystal, optical and audible illusions of many kinds, footprints, sounds, whispers . . . And it had worked, at last.

Presumably, he had believed, as they intended him to, that they *could* break through, and would, that they were playing with him. He had surrendered, returned to them.

He should have returned cowed. But he was arrogant, and cheerful.

Izvire recalled a curious doubt. Tracking him, wolf-like, through the shadow-place where he hid, fastening on an appearance and an aura she took for his, she had suddenly become aware of error. What it was she had not been sure. The moon trance had been on her. She was a huntress, certain of her quarry, and the feeling of wrongness had thrown her. Then she had seemed to lose him, and then to find him again, and had pursued him through the medium of the Crystal until the red sun magic had blocked her path. Zaister's mage-craft was very strong. Luckily he had not realized how strong, and so had given up. The sun magic had weakened the power of the priestesses working second-hand through illusion. They had withdrawn. Afterwards, Izvire had forgotten the moment of confusion, when the quarry had seemed in two places at once. Until Zaister himself had so boldly reminded her: 'I'm not Zaister. You should know. You went by me in the dark, seeking him.'

Kyrast stepped away from an iron chest. She handed a small packet to Izvire.

'Use this. A pinch, no more.'

In her mind, Izvire glimpsed a man's body falling, screaming, through black air towards red light. She shut her mind to the picture, and took the packet.

'And my daughter?'

'Strange,' said Kyrast. 'You never loved your father. Did you?'

'I don't remember him,' Izvire said. It was a lie. She did, just, remember. His handsome face, the fear in his eyes. He had visited her sometimes, but he had been diffident, nervous. 'Did *you* love him?' she said to Kyrast.

'I loved them all,' said Kyrast drily. 'Which is why I've no love left in me now. It died eight times, my love. After that, love stays dead.'

To the north of the Temple was a sloping lawn of black flowers. Trees with white bark, that had shed their leaves by this season, were hung with silver bells that chimed in the light wind.

Izvire stood on the slope, the nurse and the guard of girl companions standing about forty feet away as she had instructed. Izvire watched Vesain stamp irritably through the flowers, talking to the mechanical bird.

Izvire had been making an effort to get to know her child. She had taken her riding, she had played with her in the Moon Garden. She had brought her today, unwisely, to the Temple. Vesain was not friendly. When Izvire asked her what she would like to do, Vesain said she would like to go back to Zaister.

In thirteen days, Zaister would die.

That thirteenth night would be, as always, a long dark before moonrise. The evening would begin with feasting and flowers. A little before midnight the moon would

162

ascend in the east. A golden chariot would be brought. Scarlet beasts would draw it, lions and tigers would frisk about it. In the light of torches, the Sun's Son would be borne beyond the city, east of midnight, to meet the rising moon. And when he reached the Place . . .

Izvire found she had hidden her face in her hands. She was amazed at her own reaction. Something inside her was shouting: No, this must not be! I will not let it be!

For twelve days, since Zaister's return, Izvire had been conscious of a mounting painful tension within herself. She had thought it was grief and worry. It was not. It was the two halves of herself fighting. One half knew she could do nothing to prevent Zaister's death. The other half knew that she must.

Her head ached. She leaned on a tree, beating her fist furiously on its trunk.

'What's the matter?' said a voice.

Izvire looked down and saw Vesain peering at her with inquisitive concern.

Izvire thought of Kyrast. Izvire, too, would grow old and withered and loveless. And Vesain. And Vesain's daughter.

'We're going to see Zaister,' said Izvire.

Vesain nodded.

'Good.'

The king and her daughter entered the Sun's House. Izvire reasoned that perhaps Zaister would be secluded in the tower once more, and not come down. But he came immediately.

He looked pale and very tired, but amused and friendly.

Vesain walked solemnly up the length of the Great Room and gazed at him. Zaister bent and swept her up and swung her round in a wide arc. The silence burst into Vesain's fragmentary squeals. Zaister stopped whirling the child and put her on his shoulder. She sat there like a small black owl, staring about complacently. She held the gold bird in one hand, some of Zaister's long hair in the other. Zaister walked back towards Izvire.

'No more sorcery,' said Zaister, 'I've finished what I was working on.'

Izvire watched him. Suddenly, her tension relaxed. She stopped fighting with herself. She said, 'You have thirteen nights, twelve days. You can get away. Use your sorcery to effect a disguise. Alter the colour of your hair. Beyond the forests and the hills are mountains, and beyond those, wild country. These far lands are unknown, and no doubt their ways are sufficiently unlike ours and their methods of sacrifice different. Avoid the eastern cities. No one will suspect a stranger if he makes himself dull enough. By the time the hour of sacrifice is due you can be miles off. If you sense pursuit, enter that shadow-place where you took refuge before. I'll tell you now, Zaister – though the priestesses could trace you there, they could not follow. You were safe. You never knew this; now you do know. Remember it. So,' she said, 'leave here as quickly as you can. I can hide your absence.'

'Can you?' he asked. He was expressionless.

'Yes. I will say I've seen you, spent time with you. No one questions the king in such matters. I'll lie for as long as I'm able.'

'What about your religion?' he said. 'What about the people's trust placed in you? If I don't die, the darkening of the sun and the upheavals of the earth?'

'Oh, it's nonsense. I've always known as much. There have always been disasters, whether the consort dies or not. And we've survived them. No. You're not going to die. I've decided.'

'And what about the uproar, when they notice I've gone?'

Her face hardened.

'I'll deal with it.'

He grinned. 'Yes, I think you could.'

'Listen, Zaister,' she said, 'be serious. I don't speak lightly. It isn't a game. You must make your preparations and get away as swiftly as you can. Recollect, at full moon I will come into the Temple, crying for your blood as the rest will. Then I will be no longer Izvire, but only the sorceress, the priestess. I'll go hunting, and if I find you, I'll kill you. So tell me nothing of your plans, and fly this place and from me. I, too, am a Daughter of Night.'

He had stopped smiling.

'Yes. Of course. I can't trust you, can I?'

'No. Only now you can trust me. A few days . . . the ritual is inbred in me.'

'Then maybe I shouldn't see you again,' he said.

Her eyes were steady. Too steady, fiercely meeting his.

'No. It's better not. Though I will inform the others

that you and I are often together, dine together, bed together.'

'And at full moon you'll seek me. Even though now you mean me to escape?'

'Yes,' she said. 'I shall only recall this conversation confusedly. It won't make sense. I shall be savage, intent on your death. You can rely on that. Be far off by full moon, Zaister. For then I can no longer control what is in me.'

'What about the next consort?' Zaister said.

'I don't know,' she said. She looked abruptly afraid.

'It's a large thing to take on,' he said. 'All this.'

'Don't be stupid,' she said. 'Do you think I'm not aware of it?'

'Well, only partly,' he said.

'Zaister—' she said.

'I'm not,' he said deliberately, 'Zaister. My name is Dekteon.'

'You—' she cried.

'Yes, yes,' he said, 'we won't argue it. I'm grateful for your bravery and your kindness, Izvire. I'm flattered that you want to save me. But I don't think it can be done this way. I think I'd better stay here and die properly, as a good scapegoat should.'

Izvire went white, even her mouth. She told him, in no uncertain terms, what she thought of his mockery and his foolishness. The child, whom both had forgotten, sat on his shoulder, listening. Presently the child began to cry.

The woman and the man checked in astonishment.

'Women don't weep in your world,' said Zaister.

166

But Vesain, clutching the gold bird, howled resolutely into Zaister's neck. Zaister – Dekteon – looked embarrassed.

The tableau fell apart. The three sat down on a long couch. The man and the woman ceased confronting each other in an effort to quieten the child. The child, instinctively realizing her goal had been achieved, let herself, very gradually, be quietened.

At length, Vesain, cheerful again, played on the floor, crawling on hands and knees after the gold bird as it strutted.

Izvire said softly, 'Zaister, do you know how you will have to die?'

'Something of it,' he said. 'Enough.'

'Please,' she said, 'do what I say.'

'For once,' he said, as gently, 'let a man decide his own fate.' He took her hand. 'You'll see,' he said, 'it will be all right.'

Somehow, against everything, against her reason, she found she believed him.

FOURTEEN

Death Moon

To the east of the green city ran an ancient road. It began in a grove of white cypresses half a mile from the eastern gate. The road was formed of large paving blocks, and kept scrupulously free of undergrowth – though it was never travelled save once in every five years. An altar stood at the beginning of the road, among the cypresses, a cat altar to the moon. Near its end, the road passed another altar, in the shape of an ivory mare. The very end of the road was a crash of metal, a cry, a leap into darkness, red-lit below. In fact, the end of the road was death.

The last day of the fifth year dawned, like any other. Certain trees were in leaf, others had shed their leaves, some had just begun to blossom.

A silence hung over the city, a stillness without calm. A sense of waiting.

It was a day of holiday, as were all days before a night of full moon.

No one had seen the Sun's Son, the consort of the king, no one had seen him for thirteen days. All except the king herself. She had seen him, so she said. She went masked now. Nobody could watch, through the silver moon-face, what her expression was; if it was misery, fear, cruelty, or simple smugness that the correct order of things was going forward.

The day, which was clear and golden, passed into lilac dusk. Stars came out, but as yet there was no moon.

The tables were laid in the Great Room of the Moon Palace for a feast. The priestesses entered like black crows. One carried a black crow on her gloved fist – Kyrast. Tonight she wore the horned headdress of a High Priestess.

The king came into the chamber. She sat in the ivory chair. Wild music struck up. The alabaster lamps blazed. The consort came through the doors, the Sun's Son.

Izvire started as if she had not expected him.

He wore cloth of gold, edged with deep red silk, like blood. He crossed the room, smiling about him at the salutes and the raised goblets lifted to honour him, and sat down on the bronze chair by the king.

Below the music, below the toasts, Izvire said very softly, for his ears alone, 'I haven't seen you for two days. I thought you'd come to your senses and obeyed me. Why didn't you escape? Why are you here?'

The Sun's Son went on smiling. 'Why do you suppose?'

Something in his tone, or something in his smile – what? – made Izvire turn to stare at him. She drew off her mask. She looked ill, and slightly mad.

'Then there's nothing I can do,' she said harshly. She

lifted the goblet from a Pallid's tray, and handed the wine to her husband, Zaister. 'Drink, then. Drink it all.'

The wine was heavily drugged. The wine of the Sun's Son always was on this last night. But he looked drugged already, as indeed he might well be. The woman-kings generally had to tranquilise their consorts in the final weeks of their lives, to keep the terror from them.

Zaister – who had so often said he was not Zaister, but Dekteon – drank the red wine. When more wine was given him, he drank that also. He didn't touch the food. That, too, was not uncommon.

Beyond the windows, the mauve sky turned slowly purple.

In the city, torches and lamps moved about the streets. There was drinking there, too, and dancing and singing. The women wore white shawls and garlands of white flowers over their darkness. The men laughed drunkenly.

An hour before midnight, a new wine was served in the Great Room of the Moon Palace. The wine was black, and it was offered only to the Sun's Son. It was the one occasion in his life when he was permitted to break the colour taboo.

The wine symbolised his death. But Zaister drank it, as he had drunk the other.

Presently, escorted by the priestesses and Izvire's girl guard, the Sun's Son went out of the Palace, through the Moon Garden, into the street.

He was borne along by a press of people. Their faces, like the music which still played about them, were wild, touched, like Izvire's face, with madness.

The women and men of the city ran behind, with

170

their garlands and torches and their singing. The whole procession was on foot. They reached the portico of the Moon Temple, and Kyrast led the way inside.

This time the priestesses conducted their mystery in public. They formed a circle about the altar. Kyrast stood to the right of the altar, Izvire, the king, stood to the left. The Sun's Son, Zaister, accompanied, or guarded, by palace women, was outside the circle, among the pillars. People crowded at the door. The music and the singing stopped, and only the torches crackled.

The light dimmed, the torchlight seemed unable to penetrate as far as the altar and the female circle which contained it. The figures of the women became shadowy. The air about them seemed to fragment . . . like something seen at the bottom of a pool of unclear water, or through gauze or mist; that was how the women looked now.

Fires rose from the altar, smokes and scents. The Temple was filled by a faint rustling of invisible leaves, the timbre of invisible chimes.

It could be seen now, however indistinctly, that the women were no longer merely women. Their faces gleamed and their features blurred in the gleam, as if flame melted them from within.

A new thing appeared on the altar. A cool sphere of light, an illusory moon. It drifted upward, into the roof of the Temple, and the crowd held its breath. Then, from the top of some watchtower, a bell rang, notes like spears falling through the silence.

A voice shouted somewhere far off. The shout was taken up, borne nearer: *The moon is rising*!

Kyrast raised her gleaming withered face.

'Eastward,' she said. She pointed at Zaister. 'Go eastward, east of midnight, towards the rising of the moon.'

Zaister's face was colourless. His jaw was slack, his eyes half-closed.

Izvire's face was all glow, all white flame. Her eyes had become as vacant as the eye-slots of her mask. She walked out of the circle, out of the unclear water of the mist of the spell, yet she seemed to bring the murk of it with her.

Izvire was cruel, truly and completely cruel, for her sanity was gone, driven away by magic.

She came to Zaister and kissed him on the mouth.

No one needed to receive the pressure of her lips to know how icy they were.

She took Zaister's hand, and it would be hard to tell which hand was colder or felt less human. Together, Sun's Son and Moon's Daughter turned about and walked across the Temple, and the people fell aside before them. Zaister and Izvire, both moving like clockwork, walked towards the door.

The roadway beyond the door was clear of people, who had pressed up on the pavements and against the walls. On the roadway stood a chariot of gold, with six scarlet horses in the shafts. The horses were horned and had the feet of bears. They were garlanded, and the chariot was garlanded.

As Zaister came from the Temple, garlands were thrown about his neck, but he did not appear to notice, and walked leadenly and blindly on towards the chariot.

The scarlet horses stamped. A female groom held the reins patiently, waiting for Zaister. Zaister let go of Izvire's hand, mounted the chariot, accepted the reins. A golden whip was handed him. He stared at it. He opened his mouth as if to cry out, and instantly there came a clash of cymbals, thud of drums, wail of flutes. The crowd shrieked. Firecrackers shot into the sky and exploded in searing splinters over the starry dark, for the moon was not yet visible, save from the towers.

Izvire the king, sorceress and priestess, grinned. Her grin was frightful. It showed none of the despair which would drown her later. Izvire snapped her fingers, and the chariot horses reared, snorted fire from their nostrils, and plunged forward along the road. Eastward . . .

What now, Zaister-who-is-really-Dekteon? Drunk, drugged, bound by ritual and spell, carried to death in a chariot out of control – what now?

Dekteon–Zaister looked as if he were screaming. But the scream was silent. He clung to the reins. The impetus of the racing horses held him forward, yet balanced. In fact, he balanced perfectly, yet did not seem to know what he was doing. His hair blew backward, and his cloak from his shoulders. The manes blew back from the heads of the horses, and tendrils of steam from their nostrils. The horses were not flesh and blood. They were doll-things, machines, just as the Pallids were. There was a reason for this. Only the Sun's Son must die tonight, under the eye of the full moon. No other creature must perish with or because of him.

The broad thoroughfares of the city were thronged. The people clamoured as the chariot approached.

Frequently a yelling streamer of men and women – mainly women – would detach itself from the throng and run after the chariot. Garlands, shawls, hands, hair and the prolonged ribbons of torches swirled about the Sun's Son, but quickly fell away, for the chariot was moving very fast. No sooner had one detachment dropped behind the chariot, however, than more of the crowd broke free to chase it.

Then, towards the east gate of the city, there were fewer people. When the chariot burst into the last street that led to the gate, that street was empty. The gate, its doors wide open, was empty also.

Outside the gate stretched the midnight countryside. Unobscured by walls and towers, the moon could be seen, a perfect face, like the faces of the insane priestesses, gleaming and incorrigible.

The mechanical horses flung themselves forward as if they actually meant to reach the moon, dash at it, collide with it.

Trees spun by, branches snapping like brittle jaws in the wind of the chariot's passage. Blossoms and leaves rained into the chariot. Mouth wide, eyes wide, Dekteon–Zaister stared at the moon, leaves caught in his hair.

About a minute after he had come from the gate, the animals started to arrive.

They evolved, in sudden shapes, from every direction. From copses, groves; from beneath shrubbery, bounding lightly down from trees, loping out of tall fields of flowers. As the women and the men from the crowd had done, the animals ran towards the chariot, and after it. Unlike the women and men of the crowd, the animals were able to keep up.

The chariot rushed eastwards; the animals bounded alongside, a band of sinewy tigers to the left. Blue hares hopped to the right, a sickle-horned badger, large as a bear, lumbering among them. More distantly, came the dim flare of white flanks as a lioness emerged from the darkness. Little things scampered and squeaked, great things galloped, their strong limbs going like tireless engines, making the ground vibrate.

The spell of the priestesses had called them, set them running beside the chariot. They herded the man who must die towards his death.

Through a grove of ghostly cypresses the chariot sprang, past a cat altar, on to the wide paved eastern road which was used only once in every five years.

The silent cry, which all this while had held open the mouth of the man in the chariot, broke free of him. It was a despairing cry, a howl of submission rather than fear. And the priestesses who watched this ride in their black Vision Crystal, seeing and hearing the cry, cried out, too, in fierce triumph.

The chariot went even faster on the excellent surface of the road, and the road shot eastwards straight as a rule. The moon was higher now. Gouts of fire exploded from the nostrils of the charging horses. But the real animals ran only a short way on the road. In twos and threes they slowed, and stopped. At last, all the beasts were left behind, as all the humans and all of the city had been left behind. Even the land seemed to be withdrawing and falling back, for now the road lay over a bare rocky plateau, without vegetation or trees. Just the road now, and the chariot and the man, and the moon, and the night he was carried into.

What now, Dekteon-in-the-body-of-Zaister? Where is the miracle you meant to perform? The cunning sorcery by which you were convinced you could outwit the Daughters of Night, and death.

The face of the man showed neither cunning nor bravery. Suddenly he let go of the reins, fell on his knees on the jouncing floor of the vehicle. Unheeding, the mechanical team tore on.

There was a red glow on the eastern horizon. It tinged the disc of the moon above.

The altar-statue of a mare reared by the road. As they approached it, the team of the chariot began to jerk and lose their rhythm. They floundered together, careered to one side, then the other. Bolted.

The bolt was pre-set in these clockwork animals, yet looked convincing. Their long heads stretched out, their mouths gaped and fiery foam showered from them. From going extraordinarily fast, they seemed now to be in flight. The wheels of the chariot skinned the paving into sparks.

The glow on the horizon flickered. The rocky plateau stood out sharp and black on it.

The man in the chariot kneeled, clutching the rail with his fingers. He stared across the backs of the team, through the whipping manes, the foam, at the black silhouette which was the road's ending.

The road ended where the plateau ended. It ended in space, where the sheer cliff dropped down three hundred feet to the gulley below. In the gulley was a huge bonfire, sun-red, for the Sun's Son.

The horses clattered over the final yards of the road, and leapt out – into nothing.

For a second everything – team, chariot, driver – seemed nailed on the sky. For a second it seemed they would never fall.

And then their unity unravelled. The horses splayed out. A shaft cracked; the chariot keeled over, lay upside down on the air and started to tumble through it. Now there was a rotating wheel of metal and beasts. And from this wheel slid a man who, in his turn, became another separate wheel, spinning in a swift screaming spiral.

Shining in the light of the fire beneath, man, chariot and team plummeted into the abyss. A sorcerer, if he had, at that instant, frozen time, could have prevented the ultimate meeting between the falling man and the blazing pyre in the gulley. No sorcerer stirred, and time went on. With a dull broken noise, the bits of the whirling things in the sky splashed into the fire, the man amongst them, and all grew still.

And the flames clawed up across the cold moon.

FIFTEEN

Dekteon

Zaister – the real Zaister – woke because a Pallid was shaking his shoulder.

'No,' the real Zaister said, 'whatever it is. No.'

'Master,' said the Pallid, 'full moon.'

Zaister started up. A stab of terror came and went. He looked down at himself, and saw himself still clad in the tough body of Dekteon the slave. The room which enclosed him was familiar, fitted out with familiar things. In the window, dawn was beginning.

'Full moon when?' Zaister said.

'Last night,' said the Pallid.

'Then I am safe,' Zaister said. He shivered. It was over. The Death Moon was passed. And he had escaped. Dekteon had died, and Zaister lived. Zaister got to his feet, staggering. He felt giddy and confused. He had had a fever – a remnant of Dekteon's body's earlier fever. It had come back because – Zaister abruptly remembered everything he had forgotten: Dekteon's drab dangerous world, the hurt, the betrayal, the pain and anguish of the mines where his wits had left him. Zaister remembered

178

the rescue, the Pallid who had saved him, murmuring,
'Dekteon sent me.' The Pallid had taken Zaister
somewhere, but where? Zaister looked about him again.
He realized now the room was wrong. It was the room
that he had made to duplicate his chamber of sorcery in
the tower. The room that was in the ruined mansion in
the misty place between worlds.

'Where am I?' Zaister demanded, though he knew.

'The between-place,' the Pallid said.

'You stupid object,' Zaister said. 'Why bring me here?'

'Dekteon told me I must bring you here.'

Zaister was afraid. There was no logic to any of
this. Dekteon had died in Zaister's stead. Why should
Dekteon trouble to save Zaister beforehand? Zaister had
grown powerless in Dekteon's world; Dekteon had
apparently grown powerful in Zaister's. Why hadn't
Dekteon forced Zaister to return to the women, and
die himself?

Zaister went to the duplicate of the amber Vision
Crystal. It was not as efficient as the Crystal in his own
world. Beyond the window, he could see the valley and
its ruins, the mist lying patchily over it, as it so often did
in the between-place. Zaister had never much liked this
makeshift nowhere.

The Crystal slowly came alive. It showed him,
eventually, a paved road and a precipice. Below, a fire
smouldered greyly in the dawn. In the ashes were bits of
metal. The wreck of a chariot and a mechanised team.
Zaister did not look further. He turned away, and
presently he began to weep.

It was true. Dekteon had saved him, and then

Dekteon had perished. Zaister shrivelled at the thought of his own weakness and his guilt. At the thought of Dekteon's bizarre act of rescue.

And as he wept, Zaister heard footsteps on the stair.

He shrank against the wall. 'Who is it?' he whispered to the Pallid.

The Pallid had no need to reply. The door opened, and through the door came Zaister's own self.

It was a weird moment. Despite the sorcery each had practised, each was alarmed at this close sight of himself, Zaister's body occupied by Dekteon, Dekteon's body by Zaister. But for Zaister an extra horror was added. For this apparition he saw couldn't be Dekteon, couldn't be his own, Zaister's, body. For both this body and Dekteon had died in the chariot crash at the end of the eastern road.

Dekteon had created a Vortex Gate, as Zaister originally had, some miles from the green city, and away from the dwellings of men. Zaister had done this to avoid the attention of the priestesses until his trick was complete. Dekteon also wished to avoid attention being brought to the Gate. Though he did not think, actually, there was much risk. Nobody expected any further sorcery from the Sun's Son. Even as Dekteon had been seeking this Gate in the dark country westward of the city, he had heard the loud ritual lamentations floating from the east that marked his own death.

Dekteon reached the Vortex Gate about three hours after midnight. He passed through easily from Zaister's world to the between-place.

Once there, it was an uneventful walk.

There were no sharp-toothed sheep this time to trouble him, no herding rabbits. Just that perpetual mist that haunted the between-place, the autumnal tree-shapes. Presently he made out the ruins in the valley, and the mansion with its four gaunt towers, except that now the number of the towers had dwindled to three. As Dekteon went up the avenue of chipped statues to the door, the sun rose.

The Pallid had woken Zaister, as Dekteon had instructed it to. Zaister stood in the tower room, in Dekteon's body, and looked afraid.

'You,' Zaister said to Dekteon, very clearly, 'are dead.'

'Hardly.'

'You died, as the consort must, at the Death Moon. I saw the wreck in the fire under the plateau.'

'Yes, but you didn't see me, my friend,' Dekteon said. And both of them started at Dekteon's instinctive use of Zaister's expression.

Zaister had got back his sanity. Saved from the nightmare of the mines, nursed through his fever by the Pallid, his mind had healed. The ability to read and write had returned to him; even the ability to work small magics. His great talent for sorcery, however, he had not recovered. That remained in his body's brain, where Zaister could not reach it; the property of Dekteon.

'I never guessed,' Zaister said slowly, 'what would happen to me. I'm still mad, then. I'm imagining you – my guilt. Or are you a ghost?'

Dekteon went to the window. He looked at the yellow sky. He remembered how Zaister had once

181

looked at such a sky, and Dekteon had waited, helpless, intimidated, before Zaister's powers.

'Obviously,' Dekteon said, 'the Sun's Son died in the chariot. He had to, didn't he, to satisfy the Daughters of Night? The priestesses watch the progress of the chariot. They watch the ride and the fall. There's no chance to get away. Once the Sun's Son comes to the feast and drinks the black wine of death, he can't escape.'

'Then how—'

'Zaister,' Dekteon said, 'with your sorcery and your cunning you could have outwitted them. You never thought to, and you never tried. You preferred to drag another man out of his own world to die for you.'

'Yes,' said Zaister, 'there was no alternative.'

'Listen,' said Dekteon. 'To entrap me, you sent a Pallid into the house of Lord Fren. You made the Pallid resemble a slave, you made it speak certain words. No mean feat, yet simple for a magician who could work illusions through a crystal.'

'Don't mock me,' Zaister said. He would not, or could not, meet Dekteon's eyes, which were his own.

'No mockery, mage. Listen. I got you from the copper mines. How? I used your trick. I sent the Pallid there. I made it resemble an overseer, I made it talk and act like an overseer. And then I made it look like Dekteon the slave, and so you went free.'

'Yes,' Zaister said. 'I recall perfectly.'

'Well, then. Any good trick is worth repeating a third time.'

Zaister looked up, after all. He stared. 'A *Pallid*?'

'A Pallid,' Dekteon said. He smiled, smiling with

Zaister's mouth, in a way he was aware Zaister had smiled. 'I made some adjustments to the Pallid. I made it take on the image of Zaister, and then I dressed it in the clothes of the Sun's Son, and I sent it to the feast, in my stead. I controlled the illusion through the Vision Crystal, exactly as before, and I ensured it spoke and behaved as a consort should on his last night alive. Just the right blend of recklessness and drugged terror. My Pallid drank the red wine and the black, and much harm the wine must have caused its machinery, despite those adjustments I introduced beforehand. A Pallid, a clockwork doll, went to the Temple and out into the street, and into the chariot. A clockwork doll rode screaming along the eastern road, and a clockwork doll crashed to bits in the fire along with those pretty clockwork horses. And nobody guessed otherwise. Because nobody dreamed a man of your world would dare defy tradition, would dare to go on living when the priestesses ordered him to die.'

'But,' said Zaister. He stopped. 'But—'

'But what?'

'The decree of the religion – if the red-haired man does not die the—'

'The sun goes out, the hurricanes blow, the land shrivels, the world ends on the fifth day. But you've seen the dawn break on your world already. Come, Zaister, you don't believe this superstition any more than Kyrast the crone believes it. As for your beautiful wife, Izvire, she wants you to live. She would have insisted you escape. And your daughter would grieve for you, too, if you had died.'

Zaister's eyes were wet again. Having lived now in Zaister's world, Dekteon was patient. He said, 'What you must accept, Zaister, is that you're stronger than the women, more of a sorcerer, and at least as much a king as Izvire. If you'd only credit yourself with this, know your own strength, you can go back there. And stay there, openly, without fear.'

'How can I?' said Zaister bitterly. 'They'd kill me at once. A worse death than the other, for shirking the sacrifice.'

'Not if you wait until the fifth day,' Dekteon said. 'On the fifth day they won't have an argument left to them. When they find that you're alive, but that the sun still shines, the crops still grow, the world remains, what possible motive will they have for insisting that the Sun's Son must die?'

Zaister leaned on the far wall.

'I hate your world,' he said. 'It's a colourless banality, and the women of it, and the men – and my learning and abilities left me because it was your body and brain I had to use. What hope did I have there? If I thought I could go home . . .'

Dekteon watched the dawn in the valley, which was fading off into a bluish misty day. A group of the wild sheep appeared out of the mist. They were harmless now the women no longer worked magic on them, and they looked harmless. They trudged about between the ruined houses in the valley. Dekteon wondered if the sheep were actually real, or just phantoms of this bridge place between worlds which itself did not properly exist.

'Think,' said Dekteon. 'You resume your own flesh

again, your own body with no whip scars on it. You get the use of your own brain, with its store of sorcery. And there's that wife of yours who will love you with a fine woman's love, if you let her. And that kingship you can share with her. If you'll only believe yourself man enough.'

Zaister listened. He looked like a child who is being told a favourite story. Dekteon foresaw he might need every hour of the next four days to cudgel purpose and confidence into Zaister. Then Zaister said, 'If I go back to my world, then so must you go back to yours. Back to being a slave. No sorcery, no riches. No Izvire. The spell can only work that way, Dekteon. An exchange of the flesh, as before. I become myself, and you become yourself, a desperate fugitive on your rotten little earth. Is that what you want?'

'Well,' Dekteon said, 'it *is* my earth, and my flesh. I would say, Zaister, that it has to be. Either that, or I kill you and keep what's yours. And I'm not going to kill you, Zaister.'

Dekteon knew what he would lose; too well he knew. Lordship and power in an exotic land. Freedom, and the challenge of making something better from the downfall of the old religion of moon and sun. At some point, Dekteon saw, his own world had come close to such a religion, where women ruled and men died – but the road had taken a different turning. Now the hints of the ancient mystery remained only in songs. It was the men who were the masters. Maybe not for the better, and not for the worse, either. But all this was unimportant. It only served to prove that Dekteon's path, like the

185

path of his world, was a different one.

But he regretted Izvire, regretted giving up the woman he had discovered in her, where there had only been priestess and king before. And he regretted the child, too. Carefully, Dekteon and Zaister did not speak much of Izvire and Vesain.

Zaister's sorcery, which for the moment was Dekteon's, he would not really regret. He had no need of it. Let it go. And somehow, too, he guessed he would not lose everything, that his mind had been sharpened and educated by the physical contact with Zaister's brain. Returned to his own body, Dekteon hazarded he would still be able to read and write, perhaps even conjure a little . . . No, he would never again be quite as he had been. He had gained.

And Zaister had also gained, toughened by the fear he had tried to evade and which had caught him up, by the menace of death at an hour when he had not looked for it. The toughening did not show as yet. But one day it would be there for him. And not many men in Zaister's world had been schooled in such a way. Not many men in Zaister's world would be as strong as Zaister now was. And in a country where men had never had that kind of strength before, it was going to be some help at least.

Four days passed in the between-place. In the other worlds that lay either side of it, four days passed also.

For Dekteon and for Zaister, the time was full of talking, debate, silence. Extraordinarily linked, strange kindred, they were still not friends, not comfortable together. They had had to get over their shock at the sight of themselves, each occupied by the other. And yet, of course, they never quite got over it. Both men were hungry now to regain what was theirs, and mixed with that hunger was the dread of return, of the problems which awaited them, and the fears.

Neither now paid much heed to the landscape of the between-place, and day by day it grew less real. The mist thickened, the valley became diluted in it. Even the mansion seemed to lose further parts of itself. But on the evening of the fourth day, the mist unexpectedly cleared, revealing a glamour of red sunset across the whole sky.

Zaister and Dekteon watched the sun go down, standing on the eccentric battlements of the house. They had already seen the sun turn westward in the duplicate of the Vision Crystal, that sun of Zaister's world. All was calm there, no disasters, no terrors. The old prophesy went unfulfilled.

And Dekteon had seen Izvire in the Crystal too, for the last time. Izvire pacing between the shadows, crying in that way of hers, without tears, on the eve of her marriage to a new consort of sixteen.

'At midnight,' Dekteon said to Zaister, 'you'll know which track to take.'

'It was my sorcery first,' Zaister said. 'I do just remember it.' He smiled uneasily with Dekteon's body's mouth. 'Forgive me, Dekteon. Give me your pardon for what I did.'

'I'll forgive you,' Dekteon said. 'But tomorrow you won't need anything of mine. Not any more.'

'I still find it hard,' Zaister said slowly, 'to trust you. Why is it you don't kill me, and keep my identity? One would say you've earned it. To be a lord in my world. To have my woman — why not?'

Dekteon shrugged. It was his own gesture, not Zaister's. These gestures were coming back to him.

'I'm homesick maybe,' he said. 'Or perhaps too lazy to kill you. Or perhaps I'm a good man, Zaister, of noble character. Yes, I think possibly it's that.'

The sun vanished, and the dark came.

The Pallid appeared, mincing carefully along the battlements. It carried a gold flask, gold cups, gold wine.

'I'm content to drink to your nobility,' Zaister said. Once more he did not meet Dekteon's eyes.

Dekteon did not notice. He took his cup, and drank. He was thinking of Izvire as she paced through the dusk of a lost world.

SIXTEEN

Sorcery East of Midnight

Along the western causeway, between the flower fields,
a man came striding in the dawn, towards the city. The
glow of the city's lamps and night fires was dying.
Gradually the towers darkened against a sunrise. It was
day, the man's time. More, it was the fifth day, the day on
which Izvire the Moon took her new husband, the new
sixteen-year-old Sun's Son.

It was a serene and gorgeous morning. Birds played
in the sky. The land glowed with colours. Only the softest
of winds was blowing. Tigers, feeding in the flowers,
raised their heads to watch the man go by.

He was young, this man, well built and summer-
tanned. His face was handsome, and somehow not quite
like the faces of other men in this world. His garments
were very rich, red and gold, and his hair was the colour
of these reds and golds mixed together. It was Zaister.
Actually Zaister. The soul of Zaister and the mind and
personality of Zaister once more inside the body of
Zaister. Zaister complete. And yet . . . The stride was
stronger than Zaister's stride had been. The head was

high. Zaister was whistling. An old song, not known here.

The moon walks east of midnight,
The sun walks west of noon.

Zaister whistled, winking unexpectedly at the browsing tigers.

And though I love you, sweetheart,
I will not—

There were two women by the side of the causeway, like two black blots on the sunny morning. One shouted peremptorily to Zaister, 'You there! Man! Come here.'

Zaister went over. He looked at the women. Something in his look disconcerted them.

'You should be in the city,' the woman who had shouted said.

'Should I?' Zaister said.

The other woman stared at him, frowning.

'You are red-haired,' she said.

'So I am.'

'Don't be insolent,' said the first woman.

'No,' Zaister said, looking at her seriously, 'don't be.'

The women both caught their breath. Zaister grinned. It was Dekteon's grin, and the body Dekteon had used had not yet lost it. Something of the manner was Dekteon's too.

'Don't you know yet,' Zaister said, 'who I am?' In fact, his heart was banging and his mouth was dry, yet he was exhilarated, too. He could not quite understand the exhilaration, but he did not argue with the good luck of feeling it. The second woman gave a sudden cry.

'It's the dead come back from the fire,' announced the woman.

Zaister bowed.

'No, mistress. It's the living.'

Zaister went on along the causeway towards the city, and the women followed him, at a safe distance. Three or four minutes after, a woman in a chariot came up the road from the opposite direction, and passed Zaister without heeding him. The women on foot hailed her. The charioteer stopped. All three discussed something. In a moment or so, the chariot was turned about, the team walking back towards the city.

Later, when he was nearer the high wall and the high open gates of the city, Zaister glanced over his shoulder. There were many tailing him now, mostly women, and some men. They were all kinds; workers called from the fields, early travellers. There was even a priestess mounted on a red male lion. They kept an ostentatious gap between themselves and him, and Zaister's exhilaration soared, replacing the last of his nervous apprehension.

When he went through the gates into the already seething alertness of the city, Zaister braced himself for one particular sound, even though he knew that sound would not come any longer for him. The roar of adulation for the five-year Sun. Today another was due for that. And Zaister pondered how angry or relieved the sixteen-year-old consort would be at escaping his destiny of glory and death.

The streets were filled on this marriage morning, a different sort of crowd from the night of death, as if the

191

people, rather than the event, had been changed. Several were already staring. The Sun's Son was well-known and well-remembered. Besides, a red-haired man was a phenomenon no one ignored. A noise rose, flared, sizzled out in a hush. The followers on the heels of Zaister swelled. How long now before someone stopped him?

The marble road sloped upward. It led towards the Moon Palace and the Sun's House. Up this road in half an hour's time, would ride the new Sun's Son. Just as Zaister had once ridden.

Abruptly, the crowd before Zaister parted, and the crowds behind pressed closer. Down the marble road galloped twenty bronze-clad warriors. Obviously someone had rushed ahead and raised the alarm. The warriors pulled up before Zaister. To a man, they gaped at him.

Zaister thought: How soft these warriors have lived! No war to test them. They've never been hunted. Never been slaves, buried alive and without hope, in a mine.

'Yes?' Zaister asked.

The warrior captain cleared his throat.

'I'm to ask your name.'

'Ask then.'

The warrior looked bemused.

'It's said, sir, you're . . . that you are really—'

'Yes, my friend,' said Zaister, 'just so.'

The priestess, who had been part of his pursuit, re-appeared, minus her lion and on foot, thrusting between the people. She came straight to Zaister and stared at him.

'No,' she declared loudly, for the benefit of the crowd.

'This man bears a striking resemblance to the dead Sun, Zaister, Beloved of the Moon. But it isn't Zaister.'

Zaister laughed. The priestess who, despite her words, was wide-eyed, raised her hand to strike him. He caught her hand midway – Dekteon's response. Being Zaister, though, he finished the gesture by kissing her fingers. The crowd whispered. Zaister turned slowly round, still holding the priestess's unwilling non-plussed hand.

'In point of fact, it is Zaister,' said Zaister. 'Do I seem dead? Whoever doubts should ride up the east road and inspect the death pyre. There's metal in it and broken clockwork things. But no man-bones. No human corpse. The sacrifice lives, but the sun's still shining.'

There was an utter quiet, immediately replaced by total uproar. Unable to distinguish words, Zaister made guesses. Howls of 'Blasphemy!' Questions. Demands. He wondered why he was so amused. A third of Dekteon's rough humour possibly, left behind in Zaister's flesh, like Dekteon's song, forever now belonging to Zaister. Along with a third of Dekteon's bravery, arrogance, buoyancy. Well then, why not?

Zaister let go the priestess's hand, turned casually and started up the street again. The warriors floundered their horses round, trying to block his way.

'Please realize,' Zaister said, 'that you daren't attack me. Because there's an excellent chance I am what I say, and the person of the Sun's Son is sacred, so don't make idiots of yourselves.'

The spears wavered. The captain flapped them down fussily. Zaister thought with Dekteon's scorn: *Warriors!* What battle could these heroes hope to win? Fighting

193

for sugar-plums maybe, in the orchard.

The captain was deciding to form up an escort to see Zaister on his way, somewhere or other. The priestess, holding her kissed hand stiffly before her as if disowning it, said quickly, 'He must be taken to the Temple.'

'No,' Zaister said, 'the Moon Palace.'

There came then a distant shrilling of horns, scarcely heard over the riot of noise. It was the fanfare for the sixteen-year-old Sun consort on his way to wed the Moon.

'Captain,' Zaister said, 'take your men and go and tell that poor wretch of a boy he won't be needed. Tell him he can be a warrior, or something. The king already has a husband.'

He could hear how far his words carried, even through the racket. Despite the alterations in his personality, Zaister should have been afraid then. But he had gone too far, said too much. He really didn't care, for he suddenly saw that death had truly been left behind, and there was nothing else any of them could do to him, unless he allowed it.

Then the priestess spoke.

'Captain,' she said, 'dismount, and thrash this man. He's an imposter, and he's been provoking trouble too long.'

And the captain of the warriors got off his horse, and came blundering at Zaister. Residual memories that belonged to Dekteon had Zaister's fist in motion before he properly knew it. The fist cracked on the chin of the the warrior captain. The captain toppled gently on the road, among the flowers the crowd had been strewing for the new consort. Zaister's fist hurt. He liked it.

As the priestess gazed wildly at Zaister, her lion shouldered through the crowd and came up beside her. Zaister looked at the priestess and at the lion. It was the red male variety which only priestesses and women-kings were permitted to ride.

Zaister whistled the way he had heard Izvire whistle her lionesses. The lion, with a bewildered, accusing glare, responded. Zaister patted the lion's red head. Zaister put one foot in the stirrup and mounted the lion.

The belligerent crowd was past fresh comment. For the moment.

'Tell Kyrast,' Zaister shouted to the priestess, 'that there is one time when she is still beautiful. That's when she smiles.'

He kicked the lion lightly. It broke instantly into a racing speed that carried them through the press. It had obeyed without hesitation.

But it would take his world a little longer.

Izvire, dressed in her bride's robe, masked in her moon-mask, standing, cold with dread and misery, heard a commotion break out in the city.

She thought her new consort was coming. Early. A sulky handsome boy. When he kissed her mouth, she would taste the ashes of a dead man's lips. The man whose name was Zaister, who had told her he was called Dekteon.

She clenched her fists, and her bracelets sang. She had not been strong enough. She had not wanted him to survive hard enough. Upstairs in the Mosaic Room, her two year old daughter, having bitten her nurses thoroughly, stared at the walls, searching there for Zaister.

The child, Vesain, did not know, as yet, what lay before her, that her whole life would be the death of love.

Now the commotion was in the palace. Izvire, dully surprised, took off her mask, but made no other move.

The doors of the Great Room shot open abruptly.

In at the doors rode Zaister, on a red lion.

Strange, she did not suffer a second's doubt or fear. She knew at once, and ran to him. She did not even see the momentary uncertainty cloud his eyes, and when she looked in his eyes a minute after, the uncertainty was gone for good.

Outside, the uproar went on. Went on, despite the prophesy, under a clear sky and a bright sun, and in calm weather.

In the Mosaic Room there was also, presently, an uproar. Vesain, biting another nurse, got free, and flung herself gleefully at her father.

In an alternative world, a ship ran before a wind across a calm winter sea.

A man stood by the rail. A man with a muscular scarred body, a chipped tooth, two slave brands hidden under his shirt, and the wind of freedom in his dark red hair. Dekteon. Dekteon as he had been, soul, mind, brain and body. Dekteon complete. And yet . . . There was an elegance to him. And cleverness in the eyes, and something unmistakably aristocratic in the turn of his head, his hands, his manner of speech. Dekteon, with a third of Zaister left to him as a legacy. Dekteon able to read and write. And to work magic – little magics, but useful. For instance, the man who saw the brand of the mine on him, and was for telling the soldiers in the seaport. Once Dekteon was aboard the ship, and set for another land, the authorities could not touch him, for all countries had their own laws and ignored the rest. But the man had crept up on Dekteon in an alley, stunned and bound him. And suddenly words had come into Dekteon's head. When he said them, the ropes frayed and parted, leaving his hands free again. He opened one hand before the man's face. A spiral of whirling sparks seemed to form on Dekteon's palm. Not long after, the man sprawled mesmerized in the gutter, and Dekteon was on the ship.

He had said a spell or two aboard. It helped pay his way. Already they had nicknamed him the sorcerer. They had never seen, these people, the amazing conjurings of true sorcery.

Dekteon leaned on the rail, looking out over the smooth pleats of the sea, wondering what the new country would be like. Once or twice he glanced at a girl who sat with her back to him.

This girl was a widow's daughter, travelling with her mother and three sisters to the new country. They were poor and desolate. The instant the ship had moved, the mother started to puke. Dekteon cured her in five minutes by mesmerism. Now they all adored him, save the eldest daughter. She had a proud independent nature, and jet-black hair. She had taken a dislike to Dekteon. It was the sort of dislike such a girl would take to a man she found attractive. Dekteon thought he could win her round when he put his wits to it. Sometimes, she reminded him of Izvire.

197

A gull flew over the ship. Dekteon observed it circle and portion out the sky, and sail away. He remembered the flight of the black crow, Kyrast's spy.

He did not even know if Zaister had been successful. Though somehow Dekteon felt he *would* have known, now, by some sort of extra instinct, if Zaister had failed. Which perhaps accounted for the sensation of being watched, which came occasionally to him. Though who was activating a Vision Crystal in that other world he was not sure. Zaister? Izvire? No, not Izvire. And Zaister would have too much on his hands clearing the debris of the old religion. There would be no time for him to indulge curiosity. Probably the feeling of being watched was imagination. Or just a slave's superstitious need to glance behind him.

Yet Dekteon had become enough of a magician to be correct in what he felt. Two eyes were really on him. Two filmed, half-blind eyes that saw through the magic of the Crystal with a clarity they could no longer summon from ordinary sight. The eyes of Kyrast.

And she gazed at him intently, with a kind of friendly malice. He had entered her world in time to save her daughter, Izvire; too late to save Kyrast, herself, and that made her bitter. But what he had done, and what Zaister did now because of Dekteon, roused her anger and her laughter. She was entertained by the havoc Dekteon had wrought. It did her good. Indeed, she had sensed from the beginning it was not the real Zaister the priestesses had recovered, and she had believed his protestations that he was another. Yet, perversely, she had taken no steps to avert the disaster her bones had warned her of. She had pretended, even to herself. Because she had been vastly entertained. Now, with Zaister's return and Dekteon's going, she had set herself to trace him. It was her whim to spy on him a few minutes more, roving his own world in the body that was actually his. Dekteon – she hated and liked him in equal measure.

She saw him cross the deck of the ship. He had an easy confident stride – Zaister now strode the same way. Kyrast saw Dekteon was going to speak to the black-haired girl. And Kyrast the crone, for whom love had died eight times, turned abruptly from the Vision Crystal.

Her tears were invisible. As with all the women of her world, Kyrast's inconsolable crying was inside.

Another Silver title from Hodder Children's Books

THE CASTLE OF DARK

Tanith Lee

The sight of the castle struck inside him like a solitary chord. It was black. Even by day, black. Like a raven perched there on its rock . . .

Lilune is imprisoned in her castle, and knows nothing of the world. Lir is a travelling musician, wandering wherever his harp takes him. When Lilune calls Lir to her great castle, he knows that he cannot leave again without her.

But outside the walls, all recoil at the sight of Lilune, and Lir begins to see the darkness within – that he must act quickly, or it will consume them both.

LAW OF THE WOLF TOWER

Tanith Lee

Orphan-slave Claidi knows only the mindless rituals and cruelties of the House and the Garden, where ruling families wallow in lavish extravagance. Then a golden stranger promises freedom if she will journey with him through the savage Waste.

Mad tribes and strange cities, enemies and friends where she least expects them, above all the Wolf Tower that broods over the grim stone city of her destiny: nothing – and no one – is as it seems.

If she is to survive, Claidi must learn fast – hone her wits, sharpen her instinct for danger . . .

Freedom demands that she confront the Law – once and for all . . .

Shortlisted for the Guardian Children's Fiction Award.

Another Silver title from Hodder Children's Books

WOLF STAR RISE

Tanith Lee

Orphan–slave Claidi has fought for freedom and won. Now she looks forward to a life of happiness with the wandering Hulta people.

But once again for Claidi, nothing and no one is as it seems. Secrets menace her; a bewildering land of giant flowers and savage animals; the awesome Rise, a great cliff topped by a mansion ruled by a strange, arrogant, enigmatic Prince. And at dusk each night, the rising of the flaming Wolf Star.

Again Claidi has only her wits and courage as weapons and her diary as her only friend.